MONTPELIER PARADE

The house is on Montpelier Parade — just across town; but it might as well be a different world. Working on the garden with his father one Saturday, Sonny is full of curiosity. Then the back door eases open and she comes down the path towards him. Vera. Chance meetings become shy arrangements, and soon Sonny is in love for the first time. Casting off his lonely life of dreams and quiet violence for this intoxicating encounter, he longs to know Vera, even to save her. But what is it that Vera isn't telling him?

KARL GEARY

◆

MONTPELIER PARADE

Complete and Unabridged

ULVERSCROFT
Leicester

First published in Great Britain in 2017 by
Harvill Secker
London

First Large Print Edition
published 2018
by arrangement with
Harvill Secker
Penguin Random House
London

The moral right of the author has been asserted

Copyright © 2017 by Karl Geary
All rights reserved

A catalogue record for this book is available
from the British Library.

F

ISBN 978–1–4448–3623–3

Published by
F. A. Thorpe (Publishing)
Anstey, Leicestershire

Set by Words & Graphics Ltd.
Anstey, Leicestershire
Printed and bound in Great Britain by
T. J. International Ltd., Padstow, Cornwall

This book is printed on acid-free paper

For Laura

1

'The world's a frightening place.' Joe McCann scooped up a lump of minced beef with his fingertips and pushed it inside a small white plastic bag. 'True as God,' Joe says. 'True as God.'

You stood beside Mrs Anderson, cleaning the glass meat counter using folded newspaper and water mixed with a couple of tablespoons of vinegar. At the side of Mrs Anderson's head where the bandage stopped, you could see the bruising, black and blue.

'That's just over a pound's worth, Mrs Anderson. Is that all right for you?'

He didn't wait for an answer. He sealed the little bag with a string of red tape and set it on the counter like a white balloon.

Mrs Anderson's hand trembled when she reached across the counter with some coins. It was an effort for her to pick up the bag of meat and rearrange her shopping bag to accommodate it.

'I hope they find them,' says Joe. 'I know they will, I know they will,' he says. 'Get that door for Mrs Anderson, will you, Sonny?'

You tucked the wet newspaper into your

armpit and ran and opened the shop door for her. The bell over the door made a thin sound as she left the shop and you felt the sodden paper through your shirt.

'Listen, good luck to you now, good luck,' says Joe.

Mick came from the back room and stood beside him. 'Dreadful,' says Mick as he slowly ran his hands out over his apron. You could never tell if he meant something or if he was winding you up. You just weren't good at that sort of thing. He winked at you when he knew Joe wasn't looking.

They stood in silence, Joe and Mick, side by side like bookends, suddenly still, as if their last thought was important, something they didn't want to forget.

Joe was tall, fifty, or something like fifty. A face so mild that you couldn't look at it for long without turning.

There was a new supermarket less than a mile away. Mick never said anything about it in front of Joe; how it was only the old people who didn't drive that came to the butcher shop, how the shop stood between a post office and a Chinese takeaway like a jilted lover unable to account for its misfortunes.

When the glass counter was clean, you walked into the back room to get the brush to sweep up the stale sawdust. Mick was bored,

2

you heard him come into the room behind you. He stood in front of the chipped mirror that was hung by a run of rusted wire, wrapped around a nail over the sink. He pulled his comb out like a cowboy with a six-shooter.

'You ever touch one, Sonny?' he says.

'What?'

His hair was brown and thin and greasy, the fine comb easily found its way through. 'Touch one, did you ever touch one?'

'Touch one what?'

'A fanny.'

'A what?'

'A gee . . . A growler?'

'A what?'

'Are you deaf?'

'No.'

'Well?'

'Yeah,' you say, 'course I have.'

'Where is it?'

'Where's what?'

'You don't know, do you? Show me, show me where you think it is.'

You felt your face flush.

'It's not where you think it is,' you say.

'Where? Where do I think it is?'

The skin across Mick's face was mottled; he'd been told not to scratch at it when he was young, but he had scratched.

'You don't know, you don't,' he says.

3

He put his comb into his back pocket and stood with his hip against the sink a moment, then pushed off it and pulled his apron aside.

'Here,' he says. 'It's lower than you think . . . It's . . . Do you know where your balls are?'

'Yeah.'

'Do you?'

'Yeah.'

'Right, well, it's between where your balls stop and your arse begins.'

Mick was bent over himself showing you when Joe came in and told him, 'Knock it off, you.'

Mick winked. Says, 'We'll learn you, lad.' He walked out front and you heard him say, 'Mrs O'Brien, you get younger every time I see you.'

Joe looked at his watch and then at you. 'Come on, you, shake a leg.'

★ ★ ★

'That's right, Miss O'Sullivan.' 'Will that do you now, Miss O'Shea?' 'Good enough, Miss McCormick.' 'That's it now, as the fella says, that's it now.' And on it went, Mick and Joe, their voices came and went all day like a background radio.

You were paid ten pounds a week, one hour

after school, except Wednesdays when you'd mince the sheep's lungs for dog food and that took an extra hour. You'd worked there over a year and had saved two hundred and sixteen pounds.

The light had almost emptied from the sky, and in the shop glass you could sense your reflection under the fluorescent light, brush in hand. Beyond, the car lights streamed past.

It was near closing time when the bell chimed again and Mr Cosgrove, holding the amber smell of Higgins pub, nearly fell in the door. He was drunk and Joe was afraid of drunks. He left Mick to serve him.

Mr Cosgrove put his hand on the counter and fanned his fingers out to steady himself. It was only later when you thought about his fingerprints, you had no recollection of cleaning them off the glass. But you must have. They were gone for sure.

Mr Cosgrove dipped his chin to his chest and seemed to be waiting to stop swaying, his smeared newspaper pressed into the side of his old man's overcoat.

'Is it something for your tea, Mr Cosgrove?' says Mick. He stood with his arms folded and his head cocked to the side.

'Mr Cosgrove! Something for your tea?' Mr Cosgrove raised his head and gathered Mick in his level stare.

5

'Something for my tea. Yes.'

'Well,' says Mick, 'I have some nice liver there. You can fry that up with some onions, lovely. Or, eh . . . I have some burgers, fresh made. Ya can buy two, eat them yourself and give the wife one when you get home.'

Mick glanced over to make sure you'd heard.

'Have you a heart?' says Mr Cosgrove.

'Jesus, I couldn't sell you the heart, Mr Cosgrove. The wife would never speak to me again.'

'I'd say I'd be hungry after it,' says Mr Cosgrove, but Mick didn't like that.

'Come on now,' says Mick. 'I'm closing up, stop wasting me time.'

'Fucking leave me starving, it would.'

'Do you want the liver?' says Mick, without looking at Mr Cosgrove.

'Go on.'

'Do you want the liver?'

'Didn't I just tell you I did?'

'Look it, if you're going to be thick about it you can go somewhere else.'

'Give us fifty pence worth,' says Mr Cosgrove.

'Break the bleeding bank, why don't you?'

Mick reached into the tray of livers. It was fully dark outside and the cars had their wipers on. Rain clung like ivy to the shop glass. Mick dropped a bag of livers on the counter tied with perfect red tape.

'Give us fifty pence for that, Mr Cosgrove. And there's an extra piece in there for you, all right? So you won't be talking about me?'

You thought you heard Mr Cosgrove say something like 'Good one,' or 'Good man yourself.'

Mr Cosgrove pulled a pile of coins from his pocket, spilling tobacco dust to the floor, and peered into his open hand, lost. Mick took a silver fifty pence.

'Right-ho,' he says without a hint of failure. He saluted Mick and noticed you. 'All right, young sweepy boy.' His milky eyes washed over you and he says, 'You start out a sweepy boy, you'll end up a sweepy boy . . . Unlucky.' And he chuckled then.

He pushed himself off the counter and went to the door like he was walking the length of a small rowing boat. The copper bell rang, and Joe re-emerged from the back room.

★ ★ ★

You were closest to the door when the crash was heard. Time slowed, you'd heard how that happened, it really did, time slowed and you were given the accident in instalments. A

7

car horn first and then, underneath, the sound of rubber dragged at great speed across tarmac. And then the sound you'd imagine a wet heavy overcoat would make if you dropped it on a hard floor.

Mick, Joe and you all froze, like the characters in a cartoon, looked to the sound, to each other and back to the sound. You heard the wooden brush handle hit the floor and then you were out on the wide path, in the rain, the wind.

A small van had jumped the line and sat facing the wrong side of the traffic. You could hear the put-put-put of its diesel engine gently turning over. It was perfectly intact, save one lit headlight swinging helplessly by its wire. You couldn't find the driver's face, just his white knuckles on the steering wheel.

Mr Cosgrove's misshapen body lay across the wet tarmac. His plastic bag had been flung a few feet away from him; it was burst, empty. You couldn't help wondering where the livers might have been, when you felt a hand on your shoulder. You could feel the cold of the wet shirt pressed to your skin.

People were shouting. Joe was standing in the middle of the road, a hand raised to traffic. The driver from the van had emerged and was on his knees in front of it, his fist was pressed to his forehead, and with a splash on the road he was suddenly sick.

A small group fixed themselves to the path and compared what they knew from the telly, while round the corner came the flashing blue lights of a Garda car, as if it had been hiding back there, waiting for this moment. And all the while under Mr Cosgrove's head a blood pillow, rich and dark and thick, ebbed slowly from some unseen crack.

You found yourself standing over his body, bending your knees as you dipped closer. Rain collected in the pockets of Mr Cosgrove's half-closed eyes, his yellow teeth bared in a grimace, and you thought if you were to touch his skin, it would feel like chicken too long out of the fridge.

A packet of ten Sweet Afton poked from his shirt pocket, still sealed in plastic. 'Get out of that, the bloody hell you think you're doing?' Two Gardaí were coming towards you. You stood quickly, but not before your fingers surrounded the cigarettes and silently pulled them from the man's pocket.

Joe stood behind the Gardaí. He caught your eye and at once you knew he had seen you take the cigarettes. It was too late, you'd slipped them into your pocket. A Garda pulled you by the elbow to the path and when you tripped on the kerb, he caught you. 'Go on about your business,' he says.

You stood alone inside the shop. You'd heard the door chime shut, and it surprised you, everything in the shop unchanged. You were not sure what you thought would be different, but it seemed mean that it was the same.

You picked up the wooden brush from where it had fallen and swept the last of the sawdust towards a small pile you had made earlier. Then, using a metal shovel, scooped up the pile. You put the brush and shovel aside and began to lay fresh sawdust big fistfuls at a time, sprinkling it like seeds across the linoleum floor.

The bell chimed behind you, and you felt the quick rush of night air.

'Sure you just never know, as the fella says, you just never know,' says Joe, tapping his boots on the doormat that only he ever remembered.

'That's it,' says Mick.

Their voices were low and mature and then silent. They shared a glance at you and then a knowing look to each other.

'Right,' says Joe. 'That's grand, lad, that's grand, just leave it there and go on home.'

You still held a fistful of sawdust when you got to the back room. You threw it to the floor and took off your apron. Only then, after you had put on your coat, did you notice your hands were shaking. You felt the hard lines of the cigarette packet through the pockets of your jeans as you walked past Mick and Joe. The bell chimed, and you turned left out of the shop.

2

The light from the TV washed over the faces of your brothers. Their eyes shone in the dark room, vague and distant. Your father sat in his chair, closest to the fire, waiting to be fed.

In the kitchen the strip light flickered from time to time; it always made a humming sound. Cold water ran over your mother's hands as she skilfully peeled the potatoes with a small paring knife. There was an electric deep fryer she'd got years earlier. Its colour was faded and beginning to crack, and grease covered the red 'on' light, making it dim. The fryer made condensation drip from the wallpaper and down the glass in streaks.

Your mother didn't say anything when you came in, though you knew she felt you there. You opened one cupboard after another, peered inside, but really you were watching her. Finally you sat at the table. She was old, your ma. You were the youngest, and she was old.

You hadn't decided to tell her about Mr Cosgrove, and now, in the thick air, you knew you wouldn't. You would save it for yourself.

'Ma,' you say. 'Is dinner nearly ready?' You

wanted to hear her voice, then you'd be able to gauge how it was. But you had given her a way in. She dropped the knife on the steel draining board and dried her hands in a tea towel.

'No,' she says. 'Your father's not eaten yet.' She raised her voice to be sure he heard. 'I don't know if there'll be anything left at all.' She went closer to the doorway. 'The young lad wants his dinner and I've nothing for him, nothing, another Friday and nothing.' Then she turned back into the kitchen. 'Ask your father where your dinner is,' she says.

Beyond the doorway, there was only the volume of the TV. The last brother out had not turned it off. She spoke to you then, but was only pretending to.

'Paddy Power got something, sure, the bookies got it all right, they got it all. Liar, rotten liar. I never want to hear you lying, do you hear me, Sonny? Something I can't stand, it's liars.'

A year earlier, when she was too skinny, and she wouldn't eat or sleep or cry and she would chew at her nails till they bled, Dr Harwood had given her pills so she could sleep, but you didn't think she slept much.

She picked up a pot from the cooker and carried it to the sink. Pouring out the scalding water, she was lost in a cloud of steam. Out dropped a lump of bacon and wilted cabbage leaf into a sieve, and she put them on a plate.

'Has the house in the state it's in. He's a nothing,' she says under her breath. 'Tell your father his dinner is ready,' she says. The plate sat spewing steam.

It used to be different, but you were too young to remember that. Now the boys were older, stronger. You wondered sometimes if your father understood what went wrong, why his family had closed themselves off to him, shutting him out. Occasionally he would rear up on his hind legs and scatter the brothers, and the air would be clean for a while, but then by degrees thicken.

You pushed yourself away from the table and stood. You could never pick a side. He sat in his chair, his head still; you saw his eyes look away from the TV. His cigarette burned close to the filter in his thumbless hand.

'Dad,' you say, but it was too soft. You tried to fix it. 'Dinner's ready.'

You went back into the kitchen and out the back door into the shed attached to the house. 'Where are you going?' says your mother.

'Shed,' you say. She seemed disappointed.

★ ★ ★

14

The shed had a single light bulb and some of your father's old tools. Somebody was going to finish off the walls and the roof, but they didn't. Scattered across the concrete floor were your used bicycle parts, salvaged and stolen, but mostly stolen. There were nearly enough parts to make up a whole bike.

You closed the door, and your family faded away. They didn't come out there, it was too cold; after an hour or so you couldn't feel your toes and your hands stopped working. The bastard sound of the telly bled through, and you suddenly flung the spanner at the wall. It barely made a sound. They'd sit like that for hours, save a trip or two to the kettle, and then one by one they'd disappear off to bed, leaving your father alone.

Every night he checked your mother's ashtray for anything she'd not smoked fully. You tried not to catch him. After midnight you were drawn back inside, when you knew it was just him and you heard the opening music of some old black-and-white. You warmed yourself in front of him at what little was left of the fire.

'This is a good one,' he says. His eyes brightened a bit, and he lit the end of a charred cigarette. His face was different when they were sleeping.

'Yeah?' you say and ran up the stairs, the

way you'd learned to do it without a sound, your feet to the sides of the step where wood didn't cry out.

You went into the bathroom where the lock on the door was half painted over and could only be half closed, crouching down behind the sink to remove a loose tile. This was where all your secrets were stored, in a cavity behind the sink. You felt the old tin pencil case that held the money that would some day take you away from there, a silver lighter that wasn't always yours, and then the new plastic of the ten Sweet Afton you'd put there when you'd come up to piss.

You went back downstairs and found your father's seat was empty. The compressed cushion took a breath. The boiled kettle clicked to a halt as you balanced the packet of cigarettes on the arm of his chair and quickly sat close.

You heard his flat-footed shuffle before he appeared in the doorway carrying a mug and a slice of folded-over bread in his good hand. The tea lapped from the cup with his unsteady movements, staining the white bread and falling to the carpet. Your chest tightened, and you wondered if you should have given the smokes to your mother.

'That kettle's boiled,' he says into the room and then stopped. He nodded towards the packet and turned to you. His face was hard, and his dark brown eyes had you.

'What's this?' he says like it might be a trick you were playing.

'Found 'em,' you say. He looked back at the smokes and a sound like 'oh' came from his chest. He blinked a couple of times and made the same sound again, but this time the tightness left his face and he looked old. He raised his mug high and backed himself into the chair, careful his elbow didn't disturb the packet. It was later, when you were nearly lost inside the film, that you saw him open the Sweet Afton.

You were sleepy when the film ended. Your father stood and turned on the lights. He emptied his ashtray into the cooling fire; the butts only smouldered and you knew they'd stay in the grate until the fire was lit again the next afternoon. You shifted your weight on the sofa as if you were preparing to move. He turned off the TV and says, 'We'll be leaving at eight.' Then he says, 'Right,' on his way out of the room.

You listened to his every footstep up the stairs, his full piss and then the final two steps of the landing. A door opened and closed.

You collected the cups around the room and left them in the kitchen sink. You would have washed them, but you didn't want to make any noise. You turned out the lights and stood in the blackness listening. A tap dripped in a tired way, and the rafters could be heard upstairs, bracing against the low wind. Your body shuddered with a chill, but you didn't move, not until you were sure they were all sleeping and the house was still.

Feeling around the chair, you dropped to your knees and rubbed at your prick till it hardened, while you stoked the embers of your memory. Miss Gill, when she bent over to pick up her shopping. That ad on TV with the girl in the bathing suit. Finally you settled on Sharon Burke, where her brown legs met at the base of her miniskirt. There was only the sound of your breathing, as her hand roughly took your prick. Her eyes were as remote as the pictures in a magazine. You lifted her skirt and held her so tight it hurt you both. Her breath laboured like yours, and in a final shudder you felt the warmth spill across your hand. Your fingers slow and strong as you held on as long as you could before it was gone and you were in the dark.

You lumbered up the stairs to bed, exhausted. The temperature dipped with each step. You undressed quickly. The sheets cold. You could hear the half a dozen lungs that surrounded you, all pulling at the same air. You asked God to bless them all, but it was

18

mostly out of habit now. You looked about the room, the tall bunk beds, the shape of the bodies under the layers of blankets and coats. You could see the dead face of Mr Cosgrove and closed your eyes tight, but it wouldn't go away. You wondered where his body was now. You thought about the big fridge at the butcher shop before you turned towards the wall.

3

The sun had shown great promise earlier in the morning, resting just behind the thin clouds, but as your father's white Ford van pulled closer to the grand Georgian terrace of Montpelier Parade, it had yet to show itself. Your father's hands fell across the steering wheel like a river-boat captain's.

He was a country man, your father. He came to Dublin young and had not felt at home since. Still, when he threw the steel of a shovel into the earth his whole body moved with a single purpose: there in the physical landscape he became himself and finally he made sense. It was true that men decades younger would try to keep pace and fall aside, silently watching. Even your brothers would give that much.

It was just nine o'clock, and you felt sick from the heavy lifting. You carried the tools from the car through a narrow laneway that went around the back of the house and into the garden. Everything you touched was wet and cold and refused to surrender last night's weather. You wanted to rest, close your eyes a moment and feel warm. You were worried you might faint and imagined your father, mortified, standing over you, pushing your body with the heel of his boot.

'Get a mix on,' he says as you rounded the corner holding the final bag of Portland cement, straining not to seem strained. He stood looking over the broken garden wall. Red bricks littered the grass, and a cast-iron gate hung to one side, knocked by the high winds some weeks back. A fisherman and his son had been drowned off Dalkey Bay when their boat capsized, their bodies lost, washed out to sea. It had been in all the papers.

The shovel felt enormous in your hands. You tried to mimic your father's rhythm. With the ease of an alchemist he could bring the sand, cement and water together, but you could not. You could feel his eyes on you and knew that he was only waiting to finish his cigarette before he took the shovel back.

'Give me the bleeden' thing,' he says. 'You look like you're having a fit.' You stood watching. Outside the house you were free to admire him.

It was late morning before you found a rhythm, not his, but it would do. Your body had warmed itself, and as you gathered the red bricks into a neat pile, the world was silent, laid out before you, slow and wide, punctuated by an occasional songbird and the

21

wet scraping of your father's shovel like the gentle ticking of the day.

'Who lives here?' you say.

He stopped shovelling, and his breaths came quick as he leaned his hip against the wall, searching the sky above, his gums showing.

'Who lives here?' you say again.

'The people who have a broken garden wall live here,' he says. 'Do you want them for something?'

'I do,' you say. 'I want to buy the place and give us both a day off.'

He smirked and that was lovely. He put a fresh cigarette to his mouth. A blue Bic lighter was dwarfed in his hand, he sparked it, then shook it a few times, and it took. Grey smoke came out his nose.

'It'd be some penny now, that house,' he says, looking over the three floors of pale sandstone, the perfect windowpanes.

'It's big,' you say.

'Big all right, but big and all as it is, you can only be in one room at a time, no matter how much money you have.'

All but a single window on the top floor was covered with heavy fabric. The ground floor had closed wooden shutters. The longer you looked the more decay began to show itself. Thick green moss along the line of the gutter. The plaster was cracked, and you could see into the exposed innards under the sill.

'Must be eleven?' he says. The question drifted and was not to you; his weight shifted, and he made a decision.

'Go on and get the sandwiches,' he says, and you found yourself about to run to the car, but you held fast and walked like someone whose body was heavy.

You sat almost side by side on the bricks that you had stacked, unfolding the tinfoil, biting roughly at the sandwiches.

'You'd think she'd throw out a cup of tea,' he says, his voice low, still chewing.

'Who?' you ask.

'Your woman, in there.' He says, 'You'd think a house like that, she'd spare a few teabags and some feckin' hot water.' He searched the blank windows. 'Feck it,' he says, throwing his bread back into the tinfoil. He stood and walked along the path to the door. His fist landed on the wood like two gunshots, then three. Someone moved past the upstairs window, but it might have been your imagination. Then you heard a woman's voice muffled from inside.

'Yeah,' your father says. 'Yeah . . . I just wanted to get in and make a tea, a cup of tea.' The roughness had gone from his mouth.

'Good enough, yeah.' He nodded at you as he walked down the path and sat back on the bricks. 'Jesus, you'd give a stranger a cup of tea.' His voice low, satisfied. 'That's how they are, this lot, they'd walk all over you if you let them, that's how they hold on to the money.' He dug his heavy boot into the earth and turned the heel.

You picked at dead skin on your hands, hoping you'd find a callous or a good cut. There were none, but red dust from the bricks lined the undersides of your nails.

A latch clicked on the other side of the door, and you and him cocked your heads like stray dogs. A woman emerged, trying to balance a tray in her hands and hold the door with her foot. 'Go on and help her,' he says, and you felt his elbow hit your arm. You stood attentive, but that was all. She came towards you along the little garden path, her eyes fixed on the tray.

'Frank, I'm so sorry, but I got a late start today,' she says. She was English.

'That's all right, ma'am,' he says. 'But for the sambos get a bit dry without it.' Her fair hair blocked her face, but you already knew the smile rich people gave when they talked to someone they thought stupid. He stood up as she came closer. 'Take the tray,' he says to you, but you didn't, you stood motionless.

Her head rose up, and without meaning to be bold, you let yourself look at her.

She wasn't old at all, not in the way you'd expected — it surprised you — but she wasn't young either. She was beautiful.

'Oh,' she says, noticing you beside your father. Her eyes were green and worn in, like she was watching from a big room behind them.

'And who is this?' she says to your father, her voice like a newsreader's.

'Oh, that's me lad,' he says, and his stout figure was transported to a market day out west, standing in the mud and shit, tipping his hat to a passing carriage.

'Hello, lad,' she says with a faint smile. 'I'm afraid I've not brought you a cup.'

'That's all right, ma'am,' says your father. 'He's fine without.'

'Are you fine without?' she says;

'Yeah,' you say, quick to agree. She stepped towards you, passing the tray, her smile lines still showing, and for a moment you knew how she smelled.

'There's a few biscuits there — not the good ones I'm afraid, I've not been out.' She lowered her head and searched around her feet.

'Oh, thanks, ma'am,' he says, then stared in silence. She pushed her hand into the pockets of what you assumed to be a man's bathrobe. Sizes too big, worn and tartan; the kind old men wear in hospitals. You could see the flesh of her hand through a hole in her pocket where her finger had scratched from the inside a thousand times and broken through.

'How's the work going?' she asks.

'Good now. Won't be long getting done.'

She looked at the wall a moment, the way you might look at a jigsaw puzzle you were never going to do. 'Great,' she says, and there was more silence. She looked at you again, this time in a lazy way. 'Good of you to give your dad a hand today.'

'Oh, he's a good one all right, smart too, not the building for him. He's a good job up in McCann's butcher's during the week after school. Smart all right, get a trade indoors.'

You couldn't look at her then. You could feel a burning across your face. Shut up, shut up, shut up, you thick culchie bastard.

'It's a good profession,' she says simply and without interest, and turned and glanced at the back door.

'Good all right,' says your father.

'Well, I'll leave you two to it,' she says.

'Good enough, ma'am.' He sat back on the pile of red bricks.

'Oh,' she says. 'If you need the toilet, it's through that door, up the stairs and . . . ' She paused. Her hand fluttered in the air. 'Yes . . . first door on the landing to the right.' Her smile landed in the middle of you both. And silently she went back along the little path, inside.

'Stop gawking like an eejit,' you heard him say. 'Pour that tea and sit.'

The tray was wooden, smooth and lovely to touch. You set it carefully on the grass and poured his tea from an old-fashioned teapot. Your father fingered through the biscuits on a small plate that looked to be from the same set. He picked one up and held it under his nose, then flung it back with such force that it skipped off the tray.

'She didn't kill herself with that spread, did she?'

You left the biscuits untouched even though you wanted one.

'Weak piss,' he says after the first sip.

The blue sky only held until late afternoon, but even then when the clouds came dark and low, it didn't rain. On the hour, you heard the coast train stopping at Seapoint before moving on towards Howth or Bray. Your father said nothing. You watched him carefully. He took off his shirt and used it to wipe under his arms and neck, packed sinew and muscle moving just beneath his skin, sallow and scarred.

The work day was ending when you heard

him hum a faint, nameless tune. It lifted your mood. He told you to start cleaning up. It was two hours before the bookies closed and now he was in a hurry to leave.

'Bring that tray back in to her,' he says. He was standing stock-still, looking at the great house. The pennies you'd pay for his thoughts. 'Go on,' he says.

As you bent and picked up the tray you saw a string of tiny ants leading from the grass along the rosewood, ending at the untouched biscuit.

'I need the toilet,' you say.

He looked at you and exhaled. 'Just go behind the wall there, like I did.'

You felt your shoulders shrug.

'Take your shoes off before you go in there — be quick about it.'

When you got to the granite step, you dipped and pulled your boots from the heel. Your socks were wet, grey-white, and a blackened toenail was exposed on one side. You used your shoulder to push open the heavy door, and the first step on the cold flagstones chilled your feet. Narrow splinters of afternoon light found their way through the gaps in the shutters, burnishing here and there the contours of the kitchen. You found an old Belfast sink and unloaded the tray into it, putting the biscuits into the bin, and later you thought about her finding them.

In the hallway, stronger light filtered past stained-glass panels above the main door and a patchwork of amber, red and blue inched across the floor. The walls were high, the cornices seemed to float, and the pictures on the walls were not pictures of the pictures, even you knew that. The sound of your own movement up the stairs disappeared into the carpet. You found the bathroom following her directions: top of the stairs, first on the right.

Once locked inside, you finally admitted to yourself that you didn't need to be. You were there to discover her, as if in the stacked white towels, the pile of books on the floor, or the assorted toiletries, both gilded and plain, she could be found. There was an ink drawing without a frame, hanging from a single thumb-tack: a large woman, naked, drawn from behind, her head turned. Her eyes found you. Your fingers traced the outline of the ink, every curve, every curve. You wondered if she was still home or if every room in the house was like this, empty and full of her at the same time.

You didn't wash your hands, instead you ran the tap and watched how the rising steam fogged the mirror, just a little, just enough to blur your reflection.

The lock made a steel popping sound even though you took great care to be quiet. Pat,

pat, pat down the stairs without a whisper. You knew that the way to your father was back through the kitchen, but in the hallway off to the left a door was open. You stood completely still, comforted by the fullness of the silence as it settled around you like water in the bathtub.

A few easy steps, and you were standing inside the doorway watching her. She sat on a worn blue couch, facing into the room, her elbows stuck to her knees and her head resting in the pocket of her hands. Not reading or sleeping or even allowing her shoulders to rise with her breathing, just staring, like the way you'd watch telly, but there was no telly. Her old bathrobe had been replaced with a soft red sweater and a dark wool skirt that ran just past her knee.

Without remembering your place, you say, 'Are you not feeling well?' At first she didn't move, then she turned and you could see one of her eyes, and she laughed a little, but just with her breath. Keeping the same half-smile, she says, 'I feel fine.' There was a joke in there, but it was only for her.

You wondered if she had heard you come in and traced your movements throughout her house. 'I don't want to be a butcher,' you say. You rubbed your fingers together and they were numb.

'No?'

'No,' you say.

'What do you want to be?' she says.

'I don't know,' you say. 'I want to go away, leave here . . . Ireland, I mean, leave Ireland.'

'Where would you go?' she says, and you heard the sudden blaze of a car horn outside, and you knew it was him, missing the 4.10 at Cheltenham.

'I don't know,' you say and felt you needed to pick somewhere, anywhere. 'Maybe Barcelona,' you say then because, in case she asked, you knew that it was in Spain.

'Well,' she says. 'Maybe you can move to Barcelona and become a vegetarian.'

You looked away, unsure. The car horn again, longer this time.

'You have a beautiful face,' she says, but you didn't think she was trying to be mean. Your face felt suddenly hot.

'I think that's me da,' you say.

'I think so too,' she says, turning back into the room. Her hair spilt forwards, and you saw her white neck. You stepped backwards, out the door, through the hallway, across the kitchen and outside into the still-light garden. You were running towards your father.

4

You could hear the car engine making that tick-tick-tick cooling-down sound.

'That's one fifty, one seventy. One seventy-five.' In the front seat beside your father, your hand held out as he counted coins into it. Cars passed, and a scatter of children could be heard somewhere, laughing.

'That's three fifty, four.' He dug around in his front pocket searching for more coins, staying away from his back pocket where he kept his roll of notes. You lowered your hand to seem as if you didn't expect any more; you had learned to be grateful for any amount, you always got more that way.

He found another fistful, more than he wanted to give over, you knew that, but he could never put them back now that he'd shown them.

'Here,' he says and put the whole pile of coins in your palm. 'Here, now listen,' he says. 'Hide that from your mother.' It was more than six pounds, maybe seven, guessing by the weight. You wouldn't count it until you were up the road and out of his sight.

'Thanks, Da, thanks.' It was wrong to put

the money straight into your pocket. You weren't sure why, it just was.

You were done with each other then, itching to take leave of each other's company. The car was parked beside the bookies, and there were the notes in your father's back pocket. For a moment you thought about your mother at home and that awful look when she worried. You thought about her chapped and hardened hands. She did so much.

'You were a help today,' he says. You almost said thanks but didn't. 'Jesus, but she was a posh one, huh? I'd say a silver spoon there all right.'

The sun had dipped below the slate rooftops so slowly that it seemed to be clawing to hold on. A bus went past, and the car rocked a little. You wanted to have that easy way with him, that easy way that men have. 'Oh, silver spoon is right.' That's all you would have had to say, then laughed. You thought about her, her name, what was her name? You couldn't ask him. She'd never once looked at the hole in your socks, and she must have seen it. You remembered then that she wore a gold chain around her neck and wondered if it had a crucifix at the end of it. She'd fingered the chain absent-mindedly when she looked at you.

'She was nice,' you say. But not like you

were committed to it, not like you'd fight for it.

'Nice me arse,' he says quickly. He looked out the car window, his eyes rolling over the Paddy Power sign as if for the first time. 'Nice? A few biscuits . . . She got you cheap enough? Huh?'

'Suppose,' you say.

'Suppose is right,' he says and looked at you once before his hand reached for the door handle. 'Not a word now,' he says, and the car trembled when he got out. You did the same, the coins still in your hand, looking back just once and catching his eye by mistake.

5

Walking home across the green through the thickening dusk, you saw your mother's shadow at the window, behind the net curtains, trying to hide. You knew she had been there for hours.

'Where's your father?' she says as you cleared the doorway and you felt her fingers lock around your wrist.

'Don't know,' you say.

'How could you not know, weren't you with him?'

'Yeah.'

'Well?'

She was small, your mother, not more than five feet.

'He just dropped me at the corner,' you say.

'Did he go to the bookies?'

'Don't know.' Her grip held you in place. You knew you could push past her but not without being rough. Your eyes fell on the wool pattern of her cardigan, the blended strands of pink and grey and white. At the elbow where the wool pulled tighter, her skin showed underneath.

35

'Did he get paid?' she says.

'I don't know.'

'Did he pay you?' she says, and you were lost.

'No.'

'Bastard,' she says, letting go of your arm, leaving you for the brothers in the living room. You ran upstairs. 'Can you fathom that?' you heard her say. 'He didn't even give the young lad any money, none . . . the rotten get.'

It was the weekend, so you were allowed a bath. The stains ran from your naked body and coloured the few inches of cooling water. Your arms, your back, your knees exposed.

You lay back and felt a chill on the inside of your thigh where the water stopped. You closed your eyes, like stepping out of your own body. The water gently lapped at your skin. Your prick was hard.

You held her to you, her lips wide. Please, she says. You could feel her press against you. Please.

Downstairs, when you were dressed, your jeans felt tight and clean. You hid seven pounds and a pocket knife in your coat pocket in the hallway, a cigarette wrapped in toilet paper and three red matches too. You were unable to get all the dirt from under your fingernails and were no longer proud of it.

It was after six, and the bookies closed at

six. Your father would lose, he mostly did, and then there was nowhere else to come but home. You ate your dinner, the clock ticked and your mother paced the rooms, from the front window where she'd watch for his car then back out to your brothers, where they sat wordless, spread across chairs in a vigil. You ate quickly. She'd start at him when he got in, use what she could to hurt him, use you. You stood up from the table and she noticed the unfinished plate.

'Where are you going?' she says.

'Nowhere,' you say. 'I'm not hungry.' But you knew you had to tell her that you were going out; she worried, and you couldn't stand that.

'That's him now, Ma.' One of your brothers saw his car coming down the road and pulling up alongside the house. Your mother froze a second, then went to the window to see for herself. From the kitchen you heard the handbrake being drawn, the engine shudder and die. She was quick from the window back to the kitchen. She rubbed her hands like she was cold, and her gathered thoughts seemed to confuse and frighten her.

'I'm going out,' you say and propelled yourself towards the hallway.

'Out, out where?'

You had only a moment before he came

through the door. You took your green army coat from the hook, your favourite coat, the coat you wore to feel strong, sometimes invincible. You eyed the lock and expected it to turn. You couldn't go that way, you couldn't face him. You went back to the kitchen.

'Just out,' you say. She followed quickly behind.

'With who?'

'No one,' you say, putting on your coat. Quieting the coins in your pocket between your fingers.

'You're going out in that night, on your own?'

The fat your mother had used to fry the chips had cooled, and now a brown skin had begun to congeal across the unwashed plates.

The front door opened, your father was home. You heard his heavy footsteps on the stairs; he'd gone up to hide whatever money he had left. You imagined all the hiding places all through the house, every cavity stuffed with secrets. Your mother looked at you.

'Go then,' she says in a simple way and retreated into the room with your brothers. You felt the first flash of a hot tear.

Out the back door. In a single movement you'd scaled the little coal bunker and scrambled onto the eight-foot garden wall.

From there you pulled yourself up on the roof of the shed. The corrugated metal cried out in rhythm with your feet. You dropped to the other side and ran. Ran past the hall door, the white Ford, further out across the green, until you saw the first lights of the shops, heard the trucks on the main road where you folded over and filled your burning chest with the night air.

6

It was cold, cold enough to see your breath every time you exhaled. The rain had held off, but your feet had got wet running through the grass, and you pushed your damp socks around with your big toes.

'Excuse me, miss?' you say. You were standing about twenty feet back from the lit off-licence. You were careful not to step towards her; she was alone, heavyset, her face kind. She was carrying a bag, canvas and weighing enough to pull her body to the left as she walked. She was wearing a fitted pea coat, but the effect was pointless. It made you feel sorry for her, and you hated that.

'Excuse me, miss?' you say again, and this time she slowed, keeping a distance. She was wary of you. You had your coins already in your hand, two eighty, the exact amount. You held the coins where she could see them, so that she didn't think you were begging or going to hit her.

'I'm really sorry to bother you,' you say in your best accent. 'But, I've been invited to a party tonight.' She stopped a few feet from you then, on the off-licence side where the lights were brightest. 'It's just they won't let me in unless I bring something — I wonder if you'd mind getting me a bottle of wine . . . in there. It's two eighty.' You raised your hand and stepped towards her, but not too much. If you could get the money into their hands, they rarely gave it back.

She looked at your hand and then over her shoulder towards the light.

'Thanks very much, thank you,' you say, as if it had been agreed, and took another step towards her.

'Sorry, no,' she says and pulled the strap of her canvas bag higher on her shoulder, resting her hand across it. 'No, no,' she says, and you could see her eyes searching for a way around you, so you stepped back away, bowing your head to her.

It was getting late. You wanted to go and find Sharon up at Cats' Den, and still leave enough time to get into town on the bus. You'd sit upstairs, at the back, that was the best. You'd watch them all drinking and kissing and shouting. 'Tickets now, folks, tickets now, please.' Then the leafy Booterstown and Ballsbridge would give way to Dublin City, and you'd have your bottle hidden and your single cigarette safe inside your top pocket.

Another fifteen or was it twenty minutes

that had passed? Your shoulders began to buckle with the cold. Two more failed attempts and now fewer and fewer people. You saw a group of five approach, and out of growing desperation you tried it.

'Sorry, excuse me,' you say, and your own voice sounded hollow to you. Two men, taller than you, and three women. You had timed it all wrong, and although the man saw you, he wasn't willing to give up his impending punchline. After they laughed freely you asked again. They were closer then; they slowed, and their eyes surrounded you. You held the money forward, but already you knew it was no use.

'Sorry to bother you,' you say. 'But, I've been invited to a dinner party.' The blonde girl took to laugh. 'And it's just that I wanted to bring a bottle of wine with me . . . as a sort of thank-you.' The coins felt damp in your hand and you thought of your father doling them out in pieces. You thought of his way with her: *Yes, ma'am. No, ma'am. Three bags full, ma'am.*

'What is that?' one man says.

'Two pound eighty,' you say. 'It's how much it costs.'

'Two pounds eighty? Two pounds eighty?' he screamed in a fit of laughter; the rest followed.

One of the girls pushed at his shoulder

affectionately. 'Oh, don't be so mean,' she says, and as she pulled his arm and they walked on, she says it again.

'That's probably the same little wanker that stole your coat,' he says.

It was a long spell with only a few passing. When they did, they were all wrong or you were afraid of them. You began to dread standing there to watch the shutters roll down, and then you'd have to walk home, too afraid to go into town without the wine for comfort.

A woman walked towards you wearing a tan rain mac with a thick belt pulled across her waist. You could tell she was posh by her tall walk. Her boots made a pop-pop sound. You looked away. You didn't want her to feel you waiting for her. Pop-pop-pop. When it felt right, you turned.

'Excuse me, miss?' you say, but recognised it was her. Froze then and surrendered everything except her.

'Hello,' she says, as simple as that, and then she waited for you to tell her why you'd stopped her, but you couldn't. She was smiling at you. She looked over her shoulder and could see the brightly lit off-licence.

'Oh, dear.' She put her hand to her face and her index finger brushed just above her upper lip. 'Where are your friends?' she says, and looked across the empty streets. 'When I was your age, I always was the one picked to ask someone too.'

'Hiding,' you say and no longer felt as shy now that you weren't alone.

'Go on, let's have it then,' she says.

You took the warm coins from your pocket and felt your face break into a smile, until you saw how you had been gripping the coins so tight that now they'd left an ugly imprint. You saw the dirt on your nails and felt so grubby that you pitied her having to touch them.

'No, no,' she says. 'I want the pitch, the full pitch, and it'd better be good.'

'The pitch?' You lowered your head so she didn't see how you thought of her.

'Come on.'

'Excuse me, miss?' you say.

'Yes, young man.'

'I'm sorry to bother you . . . '

'The apology is a nice touch, but look up, you're looking shifty.'

'Sorry to bother you, miss, but I've been invited to a party, and I wanted to bring a bottle of wine, you know, as a thank you.' You held out your hand as you had before. 'They won't serve me inside, and I wondered if you'd mind . . . Thank you, thank you so much.' You were a little pleased with yourself; you couldn't help it because she seemed a little pleased.

She stood still, watching you a moment. 'Good,' she says and turned and walked directly to the shop, not taking the money, but calling over her shoulder, 'Red or white?'

'Red.'

'Good choice,' she says before disappearing behind the door.

You were no longer cold but stamped your feet anyway. An old woman passed, heavy with bags, and you thought maybe you'd help her if you weren't waiting. As you looked around, you felt warm to it all, the worried faces that drifted endlessly by in cars, hands cuffed to the wheel. The Monkstown church, lit up in the distance, suddenly seemed a kind building, even though they were Protestant and just showing off having floodlights.

When she came back her rain mac was open, and you could picture her inside the shop, carelessly opening the button between her thumb and forefinger. She held the bottle, wrapped in a dark plastic bag, against the same red jumper she had on earlier.

'You know one of us should be ashamed of ourselves,' she says. She was wearing the same skirt, but you had got that wrong, it was darker than you remembered, the wool heavier. 'Here, and hide the bloody thing or we'll both be done.' She was a little out of breath.

'Thank you,' you say.

'You're welcome. I hope she is very lovely, your friend waiting up the street.' She began to button her coat. 'Red wine is romantic.'

'Romantic?'

'Well, are you and the boys going to split a bottle of wine?'

'No,' you say and smiled because that was true.

'Well, have a good night,' she says, and she seemed for a second almost shy. She smiled a little and touched your arm before she walked away.

'Thank you,' you say and held the bottle like a trophy and watched until she disappeared.

7

It had started to rain, but it was the gentle kind. There were fewer cars along the Strand Road, fewer street lights too. You could hear a train bound for Bray; its engine sounded like it could smash right through you. All the while you watched the road ahead for packs of boys that would beat you up just for meeting them. They'd push you first for fun, as if they hadn't decided they'd hurt you. 'Giz a smoke,' they'd say, or 'What are you looking at?' They'd call you a queer and then you'd feel a kick from behind. Once they had you on the ground, they would exhaust themselves with kicks and punches. It was really the anger that made you cry, not the pain, but it all looked the same to them, it helped them go on.

You walked fast then, left off the Strand Road and away from the Martello Tower, away from the starless sky that hung over the Irish Sea.

You stood at the dark end of the church car park and stared across the scrub of wasteland to the lights of your housing estate. It was hard to hold your breath, hard to listen. You waited for your eyes to adjust, and when you felt brave for a moment you ran. Through the darkness to the other side of the high rocks, to Cats' Den, where a huge rock jutted out to form a natural canopy. Hardly a few hundred feet from the housing estate, completely hidden. You arrived at Cats' Den and searched around in the dark for a rock to sit on. The wet from the rock kissed at you through your jeans, and all the while you kept your hand clenched tight around your pocket knife. You waited to catch your breath.

You took out the bottle of wine and studied its label. It was a simple green bottle. Instead of a golden swallow were French words or maybe Italian words. There was no price, just a white paper scab where she had quickly pulled the tag with her nail. The kindness of that.

It was not a screw top, so you used your pocket knife to force the cork into the bottle. Its sour tang made your lips tight. You tipped your head back and took huge glugs that left you breathless. You closed your eyes and felt the liquid burn through you, past your throat to your belly and further, warmth spreading across your groin. You opened your eyes, wiped your mouth. Warm, all warm.

Time passed and a great silence descended, and you were no longer scared. It was as if the whole city had held its breath and tiptoed away.

You thought about having the cigarette, you even patted your hand across your chest pocket where you felt it, unbroken, but you decided to wait until you were in the dark of the cinema. Then you realised you had an extra two pounds eighty. You could buy a whole pack of ten smokes.

Carrolls were the best, the packets were red like American cigarettes.

You thought about her, how decent she'd been. You barely noticed yourself as you took another swig from the bottle. It never burned as much the second time. 'Apples in an orchard,' you heard yourself say aloud, followed by your own slight laugh. You reminded yourself to keep quiet and then wondered why. After all, you weren't afraid. Not until you heard that scraping sound in the distance like boots over stone. You felt for the outline of your pocket knife; for years you had carried it, but then you knew for sure you could never use it. You tucked the bottle into your coat and let your thumb rest over it. Listening, as the movement came slowly towards you, and you knew that someone was waiting for their eyes to adjust to the dark, just as you had done.

You remembered Sharon, only then, when you saw the top of her bleached head as she stumbled through the brambles towards you. Her head was lowered as if she was looking for something that she'd dropped earlier. You called into the darkness, 'I'm here.' So as not to frighten her.

'Fuck you doing here? Thought you were scared of the dark,' she says, catching her breath.

'I'm scared of nothing, me.'

'Shut up to fuck or I'll give you something to be scared about. You got any smokes?'

'One, but I'm keeping it for later.'

Your mother didn't like Sharon. She lived up the road from you, and her father had two rusting cars sitting on cinder blocks outside the house. The county council had been called up, an anonymous complaint that they were unsightly. Her dad was a drunk and wouldn't move them.

She found the biggest rock to sit on, the comfy rock, and took out her own cigarettes. In the spark of her match she must have seen the bottle sticking from your coat pocket. She looked off into the night. You felt shy then, taking the bottle out and sipping at it.

'Where did you get that?' she says.

'This woman bought it for me.'

Sharon pulled on her smoke and even in the dark you could see the billow of her exhale.

'She sounds like a fanny,' says Sharon.

'You're a fanny,' you say.

'Least I'm not drinking that shite.'

'You don't want some?'

'Do I fuck.'

She took her cigarette between her fingers and rolled it in a perfect circle. Sharon was little more than a year older than you, and since she'd left school she could be found up here most afternoons and some evenings, smoking.

'I saw Mr Cosgrove get killed.'

'You did not,' she says, excited.

'I did, right outside McCann's. He was drunk, he walked into the road.'

'I heard his head was nearly knocked off, that he was mangled.'

'Ah, no, he wasn't, but it was bleeding. From his head. The rest of him looked all right.'

'He couldn't have been all right if he was dead.'

'I know, but that's what was weird.'

'Was he not mangled and all?'

'No.' But then you thought of his face, that terrible look, and his body on the cold ground and everybody staring.

'I'd love to have seen that.'

'You wouldn't.'

'I fucking would, I never get to see anything.'

You had played together when you were

children, before she'd grown and wore heavy make-up, before she had boyfriends that had cars and wives and gold rings on their pinky fingers.

'What are you saving your smoke for?' she says then.

'I'm going to the pictures,' you say and heard yourself draining the excitement from your voice. You were lit up by the night and Sharon couldn't join you there, so you felt across the wide distance for her, still back in the plain evening, and hated that sympathy you had for her.

'Do you want to come?' you say, only because you were drunk.

'Why don't you go with the fanny that bought you that?' she says.

'I'm going on me own.'

'Course you are, Johnny-no-fucking-mates. That's you.'

'Do you want to come?'

'That read-underneath again?'

'Yeah.'

'Do I fuck, rather drink me own piss.'

'It's a good film.'

'You're some awful ponce,' she says and flicked her lit cigarette towards you.

'You missed.'

'Only 'cause I wanted to.'

You thought of Sharon, that way, your

bodies flung roughly together. She hugged her jacket around her. Her feet kicked in and she leaned forward, rocking herself there. You'd come close a few times, but you'd left off, not wanting to be one of those boys who made her cry. You looked up to see if you could find a single star or trace the outline of the moon.

'You'd better go,' she says.

'I'm all right for a bit.'

'Don't do me any favours.'

You wanted to go then. It was getting late but you couldn't face leaving her there alone and felt trapped.

'What are you going to do?' you say.

'Go home, I suppose.'

You asked her for a cigarette, she gave you one and you sat together, swaddled in darkness, smoking.

8

The seats at the back of the bus were all taken, so you sat a few rows from the front. The driver had seen the bottle, had given a warning look, but said nothing. It was bright upstairs and there was a clatter of laughter at every seat.

Two girls got on at the stop after you and then sat side by side one row ahead. They were about your age, but they'd dressed to hide it. You looked out the window and pretended not to be listening, stealing looks across the sides of their faces, to the make-up lines applied in a hurry, in the dark maybe, without their parents seeing. They laughed, showing their teeth and passing a naggin of vodka back and forth.

When the bus heaved into its final stop at Eden Quay, you waited to hear the door make that forced-air sound downstairs before you stood. Outside, there was only a scrap of neon along O'Connell Street, a rush of people, a thousand crushed cigarettes underfoot, and shouts and cries that rose up and receded across the oily Liffey.

In the Adelphi's lobby, a handful of people

stood around in small clusters, waiting. You were holding a ripped orange stub between your fingers, the only one there alone, the only one not old. Nobody stopped their conversation when you arrived, but the volume dropped, and eyes rolled over you in a lazy way. They whispered then, like secrets were being told.

'Screen Two has been cleaned and is now ready for seating,' says an old woman in a ruffled tuxedo shirt and black waistcoat, fully buttoned. She wedged open one side of a double door with her foot and held a torch over the stubs. The modest line moved slowly forward.

You took off your coat, used it as a cover for your bottle and offered up your ticket for inspection. The darkened theatre smelled of detergent over stale smoke. You walked quickly to the right of the screen and passed under a little sign that said 'MENS'.

There was the hum of an unseen generator. A tap dripped, and the light flickered over pink tiles. You shivered and forgot to notice yourself as you passed the mirror and on into a single cubicle.

You undid your pants and sat. The seat was cold, the relief of pissing. Your elbows tucked into your knees, your fingers pressed across your tightly shut eyes. Inside of you a howl of feeling started, just under the surface: an alone feeling you couldn't keep from yourself. You inhaled violently as though you'd been underwater for days, and your whole body shook. You punched the partition wall and a wave of pain passed through your arm. You pulled your pants up, swinging open the little door, angry to find that your face in the mirror was still light, still young. Your red mouth, your round soft lines of a soft face. You made a fist and punched at your face, just once, but it made your head ache.

You sat at the far aisle, towards the back, and the old velvet seat fell forward with a loud clunk. You looked for the images hidden in the beam of light overhead. Just light, until it landed on the big screen showing the last of the ads. You took a couple of slugs from the bottle and then carefully held it on the ground between your feet. Cigarette unwrapped from its toilet paper and examined for cracks, you sparked a match off the back of a chair. It took, first strike, as if it had been waiting for you all along. You were back, caught up again with the smoke and the heady rush.

Betty's round body appeared, naked, beautiful, a lover between her open legs. The great cries of pleasure coming off the screen sent one couple scurrying off in search of a refund. You sat with your head tilted to the dark, every inch of her known to you, frame by frame. You missed some of the words, but just bits here and there, it didn't matter. You understood he loved her, right up to the end, even when he covered her face with a pillow and held it there until she died.

The credits rolled, but you didn't move. You were drenched with feeling. You didn't move, not when the house lights were pushed to full beam; even the aggression of the cleaner didn't rouse you. It was not until the empty bottle dropped from your fingers and rolled to a stop that you stood.

★   ★   ★

The lobby was bright, unfamiliar. You saw the old woman in the ruffled shirt who had taken your stub. When you held her hand in yours, it felt unbearably soft.

'Thank you,' you say.

'All right, get home safe now, love. Jimmy?' she called out. A fat man in a shiny dark suit had an arm around you. He had a drift of dandruff across his shoulder, but you didn't say anything.

'Good man,' he says. 'Good man, this way,' and his arm felt nice as he led you outside. You were planted along the dark quays with the river on one side, and on the other, bodies escaping Saturday night on the last bus.

You decided to walk. It was dangerous, you knew that, but you wanted the chance of seeing the girls who walked along the canal. The streets looked the same and you lost your way more than once, until you finally met the slow-moving water. Cars crept by and sometimes stopped and waited for the girls' heels to crackle to life. They would lean across the glass and talk low and get in and get out and wrinkle like wrapping paper on St Stephen's Day.

'You looking for company, love? Then what are you looking at?' one of them says. 'Jaysus, your ma know you're out?' She laughed, and her lips rolled back tight across her teeth, her skin painted and rough as calf's leather. A car slowed but wouldn't stop. She was annoyed then. 'Here, young fella, fuck off and leave me work,' she says, watching the car disappear like a wish.

'I'm sorry,' you say. She looked at you, and with no hurry she pulled the string of her handbag across her shoulder and walked, joining some other girls who stood smoking by a bench. She lit a cigarette off the burning tip of another.

You sat on a bench further along the canal, listless, dull. You thought of the long walk home and were exhausted. Your head spun

58

and your eyelids began to drop. If you didn't open them, you knew you'd be sick. And then your head lurched to one side and you were.

The footpath rolled out in front of you. Your own feet on it, one took the lead, then the other, endless. Sometimes a car passed, sometimes leaves scraped together in the wind, but you didn't look up. When you thought of her, she was sleeping, in her warm bed, surrounded by clean sheets and soft pillows, in a perfect room, in a perfect house on Montpelier Parade.

It was like a dream, that's how you'd remember the four or five miles you walked to deliver yourself to her doorstep. You banged on her door with your fist and called to her, 'Missus.' It was loud. It felt good. 'Missus.' You roared until your voice went hoarse with the relief. A light went on upstairs, and there was movement beyond the heavy door.

'Who the bloody hell is that?' she says. 'I'll call the guards.'

'It's me,' you say. 'Me, you got the wine for.'

Silence, and then a key moved in the latch and the door opened. She stood there, light thrown around her; you could feel it on your own face, and you could feel your eyes squint.

'You're joking, you have to be joking. Do

you have any idea what time it is?'

'No,' you say. 'I'm sorry.'

'Christ, I knew I shouldn't have bought it. I knew,' she says. It was mostly for herself. She leaned her forehead to the edge of the door.

'What do you want? What? Because I'm about to call your father,' she says.

'I want, I was at the pictures and it started me thinking.'

She looked at you, confused. She was wearing the same robe, pulled in a tight knot across her waist.

'Why are you here?' she says, her voice pouring in and extinguishing you. On the long walk you'd had it, an idea, a thousand gorgeous things to tell her, but now, as you looked shyly down, every one left you, and even the lit cigarette you thought you held was gone.

'I'm really sorry, I shouldn't have.' Your foot was already feeling for the first step as you began to back away.

'Oh, for God's sake!'

'I'm so sorry, I wanted to . . . Thanks, thanks for the wine, it was the good wine. I noticed that.' She came forward and her face fell into shadow and you were standing at the base of the steps and could no longer see how she looked at you.

'I'm sorry . . . I'm sorry,' you say again,

before you panicked and ran.

'Wait.' She called after you once, then stood there a moment, pulling her robe around her. You saw from your hiding place beyond the wall as she stepped back inside the house, turning once before she closed the door.

9

'Get him, get him!' You were running as fast as you could through the brick lane at the back of the bicycle shed. You were fast, impervious to the uneven tarmac. You didn't dare look back to the prefect chasing you. Graeme, that was his name. Graeme something. He wore a cricket jumper. He was tall and had shy, sandy eyebrows. He'd been waiting for you, hidden inside the tuck shop where he had a clear view into the shed.

He may have been there for hours, hunkered low to the floor, and all the while you sat through a class, both of you measuring the lazy strokes of a clock. He had had the thought of marching you roughly to the principal's office. There he could detail the minutes of your crimes and stand proudly, having prevented them.

Before the bell at eleven you'd left the classroom. Your shirt covered a small vice grip and there were pliers jammed under your belt: you needed a front derailleur. It was one piece of hundreds that made up a bicycle, the last piece. You had to break the chain to remove it; smashing it would be quicker, but you hadn't smashed it. Instead you'd found the release clip, removed the chain, took the derailleur and reattached the chain. At least the bike still would work, unlike when you stole a wheel and later had to walk past a student in tears dragging the misshapen frame behind them.

It was a ten-speed Raleigh, blue. You'd seen it that morning the second time you had circled past, at close to nine when the shed had begun to overflow, bicycles littered this way and that. You took the pliers from under your belt; they had been painfully pressing cold into your skin, and you were sure they would leave a mark.

That's how the prefect wanted you, your hands covered in oil, tool clasped tight, bolts one by one inside your pocket, bent defenceless over the now-mutilated mechanics. He waited.

You felt none of that, how he must have thought, I'll let him get a little further, I'll let him settle in, I'll get him all right. You sensed nothing, even when he'd crept a few feet from you, and it was only when a pebble, dislodged by his foot, skittered quickly towards you that you turned in time to see his raised hand over your shoulder, collapsing your body like a broken spring across the frame.

You pushed back against him, but he had

hold of your shirt, pulling at it until the buttons gave. You pushed him again, harder this time. He lost his balance, falling slowly over the wheel of a bicycle set behind him like a trick. He tried to pull you with him, but then let go and splayed his arms out behind him, trying to break his fall. It was then you ran, hearing the elevens bell, and then the shouts and cries, 'Get him, get him.'

You had a good lead. You ran through the first trickle of students that had begun to emerge from the classrooms, through a high-bricked corridor to where a black steel gate stood between you and the main road beyond, maybe eight feet high, with a ledge halfway up where you could get your footing, and in a few rehearsed strides you were over the crest of it and dropping down to the other side.

You knew he wouldn't follow you outside. No, he'd go up the principal's office, probably bringing the bicycle with him. He'd knock on the office door and wait, assembling a story where he could be the hero. You couldn't blame him for that.

You were sorry then, as you slowed your pace, checking over your shoulder. Being caught always made you sorry, but it didn't feel like the sorry for being caught. It was the sorry that was deeper inside you and made

64

you heavy and sad and think that it would be nice to be asleep or somewhere else. You crossed over the wet road. You would have to wait it out a few hours and go back for the last class. He probably didn't know what you were called, but he knew the rest of it, and it would only be a matter of time before your name came across the intercom, summoning you to the office. It would be known that it was you, would find its way through the line at the tuck shop, along corridor A, corridor B, corridor C, settling in a dust around you, in secret whispers and looks along the classroom. You knew how it went.

10

'Those young ones from your school, Sonny. They're fucking gagging. Look it, ya'd lick the arses off 'em,' says Mick.

His hand gripped his prick through his apron, his wet tongue showing. You were standing at the partition wall, in the back of the shop, using the steel brush to clean off the huge butcher block.

'Would you ride her, would you? Look, look, do you know her?' he says. You stopped what you were doing and looked through the doorway, careful not to be seen. It was April O'Brian and two girls you didn't know. You'd sat together once in Mr Philips's class. April's hair was long and brown and brushed. She had a school bag her parents had bought for her in London, and her books were covered in plain brown paper, neatly folded and sealed with clear tape.

'Them young ones in your school, huh? They weren't making them like that when I was in school. Fuck's sake. It's the bleeden' money, you know? Money . . . They can afford to grow them right. It's the skin an' all, it's different,' he says, then his thoughts made his face soften, and he was a schoolboy again. He turned away; whatever he was thinking was for him.

You started back, scraping the wood with the steel and keeping an occasional eye on the clock. Soon you'd have to go outside to sweep the path. Customers trailed sawdust on the soles of their shoes from the shop to the outside. You put it off as long as you could, hoping your classmates would have already walked past. You knew there was a hockey game on, and that would delay them.

The steel bristle passed over the block, rolled the dried blood and sawdust into neat balls and spat them onto the floor.

The brass bell over the shop door cut in. Mick reached for his comb in his back pocket, and he ran it through his hair.

'Good Jesus, look at that,' he says and walked out to the front of the shop. You stopped scraping, rested your hands on the steel and bowed your head to listen.

'Now,' says Mick. 'That's shaping up to be a nice evening.'

Silence. Somebody was considering what he'd said. Regulars didn't listen to Mick; they waited for a gap in his questions, so they could order or tell him about what had happened to them.

'Yes,' says a woman's voice. An English

accent. 'Yes, I think it is,' she says. It was her.

'Was it something for the dinner you were after?' says Mick. There was another pause, and your head lowered closer to the block.

'Well,' she started. 'Yes, em, can I have a beef tenderloin, not too thick, slightly marbled.' She paused. There was something else, but she stopped short. 'And that's all, thank you,' she says. You stood stock-still.

'Well, I'm guessing now that that's a very happy man at home,' says Mick with a laugh. There was no answer, and you knew Mick was unsure with her. 'Just give me one second there and I'll have that out for you.'

Mick left the shop and passed you, without jokes then, towards the big fridge in the back.

You stepped towards the partition wall, put your face to the cold surface. Slowly you slid your fingers around the door opening and pulled yourself forward, allowing just a single eye past the wall until you saw her. She seemed tall, standing in that tan rain mac, aimlessly staring the way people did when they thought they were alone.

You heard the fridge door slam shut and picked up the brush in time to see Mick heading back, preceded by the cut of meat, as if it were attached to a hook and line and he was being reeled along.

'Now!' he says. 'How's that look for you?'

You wondered if Mick was right, and at home there was a very happy man sitting at that long dark table, waiting for her. It had never occurred to you, and you felt empty at the thought of it.

'That's fine,' she says. You heard the wisp of a plastic bag.

'Excuse me,' she says. 'Is there a young man working here, part-time I think? I don't know his name, his father's a builder, Frank?'

'You don't mean Sonny, do you? Is he in trouble?' says Mick.

'No. No, not at all. He's not here today, is he?'

'He certainly is,' says Mick. 'Sonny?' he called, but already he was coming for you.

'If he's not too busy,' she says after him.

'Busy doing nothing,' he says, and he was in front of you, whispering.

'There's someone out here looking for you,' he says, worried. 'What's she want?'

When she saw you, she smiled in a kind way, and you remembered how her eyes were and how when she smiled gentle lines curled beside them.

'Hello,' she says. 'I hope I'm not disturbing you.'

'Sure, he does nothing,' says Mick with a laugh from behind the counter, embarrassed when she didn't take notice.

'I wanted to make sure you were all right?' she says, then turned to Mick. 'He hurt his leg doing some work for me.' She didn't take her eyes off you and was very serious when she says, 'Are you all right?'

'Yes,' you say. Your upper lip stuck to your teeth when you tried to smile, and you wished then you'd taken off your apron.

'Do you remember my house just off the Monkstown Road?' she says with a small smile. A secret smile.

'Yeah,' you say. You couldn't look at her for long. Her skirt ran just past the knee and flared a little; beyond that you could see the curve of her calf, naked to her boot.

'Well,' she says. 'I'm going to be selling it in a while, and I wondered, if you have any time on weekends and wanted to pick up some extra work . . . It's just I have a bunch of odd jobs about the place and I don't know anybody else to ask.'

'You're leaving?' you say.

'What? Yes, well, eventually. I mean, of course I'd pay you, and only if it doesn't interfere with school or studies or anything,' she says. 'What do you think?'

It surprised you to find her waiting for an answer.

'Yes,' you say. 'I'd . . . Yes.'

'Well, good,' she says, nodding her head once to show how she was pleased.

'Do you want to just telephone me to let me know when suits?' she says, patting her pockets, and then she looked at Mick, who had drifted away but not so much that he couldn't hear. 'Do you . . . ?' Her hand drawing on the air.

'Yeah,' says Mick, suddenly spinning, the chewed blue Bic pen in his top pocket forgotten. 'There you are, now,' he says, having found one beside the cash register.

You watched her long fingers carry her name across a piece of scrap paper. When she handed it to you, you held it away to read it. You didn't know why except that you'd seen people do that. You knew you'd be free to work for her and could have told her but decided it would be better to telephone, after she'd gone and written her number for you.

'Thank you,' she says. 'Call when you can.' She smiled again, showing a small dark brown stain at the side of her canine tooth.

'Bye-bye now,' she says, and then a different 'Bye' for Mick, and she left. You watched her pass in front of the window. Past the roughly painted sign, a smiling pig holding a plate of himself.

You carried the paper to the back room,

71

and before folding it carefully and sliding it into your pocket, you read her name once, not out loud, keeping it to yourself. Vera.

11

'I got a job,' you say, and you're proud.

'You leaving school?' says Sharon Burke.

'No.'

'Bleeden' snobby eejits you go to school with. Just fucking leave,' she says, sitting on the flat rock, her knees together and feet splayed wide. She pulled her bleached hair through her fingers.

'You know the dole is fifty-five a week?' she says.

'Everybody knows that,' you say.

'You know how many smokes that is?' Her voice softened, and she thought about it. 'Lots of smokes,' she says, listless, carefully separating a single hair from the rest. The tips of her fingers had pink and red blotches. Her eyes were too pale to call blue, more like blue after someone rinsed it under the tap. She squinted one eye shut and held the strand of hair to the sunlight.

'Don't know what your ma's thinking, sending you there.'

'No bus fare,' you say. Then, 'They have to take you.'

'What are you, special needs?'

73

'I wouldn't do any better at the tech,' you say, and she laughed.

'You, at the tech? They'd bate the shite outta you.'

Your brothers had gone to the tech. Nobody bate the shite out of them. But you had begged not to go and after a discussion at home it was decided you could be sent elsewhere.

'What's the job?' she says.

'Working for a woman, inside her house,' you say.

'What, a butler?'

'No, fixing things.'

'A handyman,' she says.

You thought about it, disappointed. No, not that.

'She's nice,' you say, and then wished you hadn't.

'What's so nice about her?'

'Don't know, she just seems nice.'

'She posh?'

'Suppose.'

'How old is she?'

'Don't know.'

'Bleeden' look at you.'

'What?'

'You fancy her, you do.'

'Fuck off,' you say, but without force.

'Do you like my shoes?' She pointed to her

white patent-leather flats.

'Yeah, they're all right,' you say. 'They're nice.' She fingered the dried mud from the sides and wiped her finger on the rock.

After work there'd been enough light left, so you'd walked along the narrow path, through the brambles, the stickybacks, the nettles, towards Cats' Den.

'You like girls' shoes,' she says and laughed out loud. 'Ya big ponce.'

'You like men's willies,' you say. 'Ya big slut.'

'You big girl's blouse,' she says.

'Ya big munching fanny.'

'Ya big glass-eyed, big-lipped fairy.'

'Tart.' 'Ponce.' 'Tart.' 'Ponce.' 'Tart.' 'Ponce.' Fast and loud until it was a great tuneless noise. She lunged at you, punched, tried to give you a dead arm. You pulled her to you, pretending to defend yourself. She was solid and hot against you. You wrestled each other to the ground, your legs locked. You were on top of her then, and suddenly you wanted to kiss her, then you didn't, then you wanted to again. All the while her pubic bone ground against your prick. Sharon went suddenly limp. You released her arms, and she left them stretched out like a cross. Her eyes blinked up at you, the sun across her face, and she steadied her breath.

75

'You could do anything you want to me right now, and I couldn't stop you,' she says, and it made you sick and excited.

'Well?' she says simply.

'Well what?' you say. Your eyes fell across her neck, along her exposed shoulder, the no-longer-white of her bra. You wanted to all right, but you were scared she'd tell.

Then you thought of her taking the time to carefully hand-wash her dress at her kitchen sink. Standing in a T-shirt maybe. Her feet cold, waiting for the kettle to boil. The dress, crushed into the ground beneath you. You thought of her careful steps to Cats' Den. Trying to keep the patent-leather flats clean and failing as she'd tiptoed across the wet ground.

You thought of Vera. Sharon watched you then, weighed your every movement and gesture. And all through your body was that dreadful sadness, and just as you thought you might cry, Sharon Burke made a boy's fist and boxed you hard across the side of the face. It forced you back up on your feet and away from her.

'Fuck you do that for?' you say, reaching to help her stand.

'Prick,' she says, standing on her own.

You watched her walk back and sit. She lit a cigarette. Smoked it down to the filter and killed it against the rock, leaving a black ash stain. The inside of your mouth felt thick, like your tongue was rusting.

'Da will be looking for me for me dinner,' she says, chewing the already tender flesh around her fingernails. It surprised you when you moved over to her, bent your knees in front of her. You gripped her foot and gently pulled it towards you. You felt the muscles in her leg tighten first and then release. You put her foot on your thigh and began to clean the mud from her white shoes with the sleeve of your coat, slowly, carefully, like drying white porcelain teacups with a towel. One foot, then the next.

'You can if you want to,' she says. 'I don't care.' When you looked up at her she was wiping tears with a fist.

A blackbird landed on a bramble a few feet away. You watched it lower its head, foraging a bit before flying away. It was getting dark, and the temperature had dropped.

'I'd better go get me dinner too,' you say.

'Yeah,' she says.

A few clouds moved in from the west, dark, heavy. There were the sounds of the early evening, your breathing and the scraping of stones underfoot as you shifted your weight. Sharon stood and took a few steps and stopped. She held there a second or two. You thought

she was going to turn and say or do something, but she walked on. You lifted yourself
off the ground onto the flat rock. It held the
scrap of warmth it had taken from her. She
went without looking back and quickly disappeared through the wild brambles.

12

You waited two days to telephone Vera; that seemed the right amount of time. It was difficult, waiting. Then you wondered if you had waited too long, and you ran to the phone box after work.

'*Fuck the Pigs*' had been scratched into the cream paint of the telephone box with a knife. That would make the blade blunt, you were sure. '*Brits out, IRA*' and '*micky and bonner, true love*' had been written by the same hand in blue ink, either by Micky or Bonner.

The black plastic receiver felt big and clumsy in your hand, and you could hear your own breath in the earpiece. You checked the numbers from the worn piece of paper, though there was little need. You pressed them each carefully. Four times it rang, then she answered, 'Hello, you've reached Vera.'

'Hello . . . It's Sonny.' The sing-song of your own eager voice.

'I'm not here right now. Please leave a message, and I'll return your call.'

It was a machine and you didn't know about machines. The long beep and a space you were supposed to fill. You panicked and

79

quickly pressed the B button. A steel clicking sound as the telephone was supposed to spit your ten pence into the slot, but it didn't. The phone went dead. You put the receiver back on the hook and stood inside the telephone box, unsure. You had no more coins.

Nervously you fingered the thick leather straps that held the door shut, while the box shuddered to each passing car. You turned to find an older man leaning his back against the wall, staring impatiently.

At home you carefully ripped a page from a school notebook and took hold of a pen and pressed it like a cold chisel onto the page, and remembered how your father had tried to write a price for Mr Murphy. When the time came to write Mr Murphy's name, he had stalled and looked at the faces around him, and there was no help. You had written the name, Murphy, on a slip of paper and later left it by his chair.

You wrote to Vera that you'd come to work on Saturday. The flap of her letterbox was stiff, and even when you'd pushed past it, there was a draught stop, like two sweeping brushes pushed together. The light paper creased and folded, and it seemed to take for ever for your fingers to work it through.

★ ★ ★

The night before, you'd fallen between the cracks of sleep and half-sleep, a restless carousel, excitement, dread, excitement. You dressed carefully in the dark before sitting at the kitchen table waiting for the first signs of light to show through the clouds. Before seven you heard your mother's bedroom door open, her gentle footsteps to the bathroom, then you slipped out the back door.

It was hard to walk up the few steps to Vera's house. Your hands were damp and heavy inside your pockets, your fingers felt cold against each other as they rubbed in and out of a fist. When you rang the doorbell you could hear it clearly from the other side of the thick door. The house seemed not entirely dead, but tired and indifferent to the world around it.

A taxi drove along the road towards you, the driver's face pressed into the glass, searching for numbers. He stopped close by and started to roll down his window. You rang a second time, keeping your back to him. The door rushed open and Vera was standing in front of you. She had one arm outstretched and the other digging through her handbag, her head down, until she pulled out a set of keys and looked up, surprised. She looked past you, towards the taxi. She zipped her bag, and her head shook a little.

'I left a letter, a note, for the work,' you say.

'The work?' She looked blankly at you.

'I'm Sonny, from the butcher shop.'

'Of course, yes. Yes, of course.' She searched your face, trying to remember. 'Oh, the work, fuck. Did we say today? I have — '

The car horn flared from the taxi; her body flinched.

'Come on, missus, will you. I haven't all bloody — '

'Hey!' you shouted, hearing a voice you'd never heard before, loud enough to startle you both. 'Give her a second. She's coming.'

When you turned back she looked at you as though she was searching for something. She was scattered and frantic, holding her bag tight to herself. She'd been crying.

'You all right?' you say.

'Yes, yes, of course. I have to leave, I'd just forgotten.'

'It's all right. It's not important, I can come back.'

She'd unzipped her bag and taken out a ten-pound note and was holding it towards you.

'I'm sorry, really,' she says.

'I don't want that,' you say.

She took your wrist and held your arm in place, stuffing the note into your hand. Her fingers were soft; one of her nails pinched the flesh of your open palm.

You couldn't say thank you. But without turning from her you walked down the steps and opened the taxi's door. When she sat in, you dipped down and lifted the train of her coat so that it wouldn't catch when the door closed. You wanted to tell the driver to watch his manners but didn't. It wasn't something you could say once you'd thought it first. Through the glass you could see her mouth the words of her destination. You walked away as if there was somewhere important you were needed and listened for the taxi's engine to fade. When you were sure it had, you turned back.

You sat long enough on her steps for your body to feel the first shiver from the cold. At home, there'd be no fire lit till dark. Cars moved steadily on the main road, and a couple walked past holding hands through their gloves. The man had a newspaper under his arm, and he gave you a warning look.

You carefully flattened the ten-pound note and straightened its edges between your fingers and thumb, folding it twice before standing to post it through her letterbox. But you stopped then, putting the note inside your pocket. You walked around to the back lane, retracing the steps you'd taken with your father carrying in the sand and cement.

The lane was deserted. You checked the bank of windows for any faces that might be seen through the glass. When you thought it clear you scaled the garden wall and jumped down and walked along the little garden path to the back door. The windows were old and could be opened and closed without ever seeming forced, but you would need none of that because before you reached to the latch at the back door, you knew it would be unlocked. A gentle click and you stood inside the dark kitchen.

There was a great burning at the centre of you, and the world was somewhere else. You found you could be inside and watch yourself at the same time. On the long table there was a single plate with some toast crusts. A mug of tea beside it, cooling, a yellow skin formed over it like a crescent moon. There was a large ceramic ashtray with four cigarette butts crushed inside with enough white left on them to feed your father for an entire evening.

You touched your finger to your tongue and ran it through the ashtray; the ashes took to your skin like charcoal. When you put your hand to your mouth it had no taste though the tar burned a little.

In the middle of the table, there were two piles of books beside an array of condiments:

unknown flavours, bright colours, different sizes. It was then that you saw the bottles of pills. Four of them, plastic with white labels.

'*To be taken once daily.*' '*To be taken three times daily.*' '*To be taken before a meal.*' '*To be taken after a meal.*'

Vera Hatton. Her name on each bottle, along with medical words that you did not understand. You opened them up and looked inside.

'Vera Hatton,' you say out loud, putting them back in their exact places. That's what people remember, exactly where they left things. They forget all sorts, but if you leave an object two inches from where you picked it up, they'll tell you, 'That's not where I left that.'

The hallway and the sitting room at the front of the house faced south and were brightly lit. You knew the sea lay beyond, at the bottom of a gentle hill, partially hidden behind rooftops. You let your hand fall on the back of the blue couch. The light on your face felt warm.

At the top of the stairs you walked to where an open door poured more light across the corridor, and you stood on its threshold looking so slowly it was almost a caress. The heavy chocolate-brown curtains that you had seen from outside were open. Her bed was old-fashioned, simple wood. Mahogany maybe, dark, with just the hint of a pale blue flower painted once on both sides of the headboard. The floorboards would have been naked except for some faded white paint and a small rug at the side of the bed where she slept. At the base of the bed lay a red wool blanket, neatly folded, except for its tassels spilling over the unmade white sheets.

Here, pictures and photographs were scattered along the walls, some bare, some framed. One photograph drew you into the room across the creaking boards. A small image, sun-faded. Her face, a little younger than the one she now had, smiling. You were so close to her that the picture began to fog with the heat of your breath.

Your sleepless night caught hold of you, and you were exhausted then. You looked at her bed. You had always thought that Goldilocks was a fool for sleeping in the bears' bed. Of course they would come home and find her.

You leaned your head to her pillow. It was her smell all right, the smell her hair and body made when tumbled together with sleep. Still, you didn't dare lie down.

You retraced your steps through the house, and when you were sure everything was the same as before you'd come, you pulled the back door tight until you heard the latch click.

★　★　★

You walked the strand at Seapoint, killing time until the builders' yard opened. It was deserted mostly. The sea lapped the shore in lazy strokes and the clouds were fully white and shapeless, showing no sky at all. They seemed to fall into the sea at the horizon. The hairy man with the wide back was coming out of the water. You'd seen him before; he had the bulk of a sea lion.

You'd stood there once with your mother and watched the mail boat come in from Holyhead. You asked her how long the mail boat had run. A hundred years, she'd said, but then that she didn't know. You'd held her hand a bit on the way there, though you'd become shy about it by then. You'd wanted to ask her something else, but then you couldn't remember; it was something about your father, but you'd known you shouldn't, even though she hadn't told you. She'd never said, 'You can't ask that about your father.' You never understood how that was with people, that they could tell you all kinds of things without saying anything.

87

13

Just hours later you went back to the lane and climbed back over Vera's wall. Set out two paint cans. You scraped away the old paint, listening all the while for her. The sills had been red once and black before that, and already your being inside her house earlier seemed more like a dream than a memory.

By late afternoon you slowed the work. She was not back, and you were almost finished. You had left a few spots so that when she did come home you had a reason to stay. The sills looked better for sure; the colour was a near-perfect match. Your hand had held steady, and the lines kept straight. You were pleased with the work. That was all you had to hold you when you heard the front door open and close. You could hear the steps she took into the kitchen, and see the shape of her somewhat distorted through the old, uneven glass.

You were about to knock on the window to warn her you were there, so as not to frighten her. Your hand had already formed a fist, with your middle knuckle ready. But you held back. She was a blur of speed and determination. It was as if she were bursting for a piss, that way the body takes over and anything that won't serve that relief falls aside.

She took off her coat and draped it over a chair, then went to a cupboard and took out a bowl, setting it on the table. She's hungry, you thought, she's just hungry. She had forgotten about breakfast, the same way she had forgotten about you, and for a moment you felt better about having been forgotten.

You raised your hand again to the glass, but again held back, because just then she opened the first of the brown tablet bottles and poured them. You could hear each tiny pill tap against the ceramic bowl, like nails falling on a tiled floor. She opened a second bottle, then a third.

The strap of her handbag was stretched over the same chair as her coat. You could hear the sound of the zip. She took out a plastic bag, folded over itself again and again. She unfurled it flat across the table, reached in and found another brown bottle.

Vera, as if suddenly sensing you, looked towards the back door. You crouched to your knees. She would look to the window next, you were sure.

Beneath the sill you felt the cold from the wet wall pressing into your back. You pushed your forehead into your knees and your hands through your hair. Fingertips pressed down to your scalp, moving your roots, making a loud scratching sound inside your head.

The day before, you'd walked home from the butcher shop and passed some young boys grouped around a dead dog. One of them was poking at its head with a stick. The boys were silent. You wondered if the carcass would be left out to decompose or if someone would come and remove it. Who? Who would come? You imagined a wasteland of things dead, dogs, cats too, fish, their iridescence fading like when you take a pebble home from the beach.

You looked out along the garden to your father's wall, the little gate, half open, level now. He had got that right. You shifted the weight on your feet and could feel the wet paint pulling at your back like Velcro. Your ma would kill you.

You heard scraping, the legs of a chair being pushed over the flagstones. A tap ran, cold water out of the freshly painted pipe just to your left. It ran for a while. Was she standing at the sink, with a glass in her hand? You heard the same scraping sound, she was sitting back down. And then, save a few drips and drops beside you, silence.

'Goodness, it does look a lot smarter.' That

was what she was supposed to say, having gone past the initial shock of finding you in her garden. After you'd directed her attention to your work, she'd have been delighted. You'd have asked for a brush to sweep up the stray paint chips and when she brought it to you she'd have insisted on you staying for a sandwich and a cup of tea. You'd have swept the paint chips and they would have danced like fairy dust in the breeze.

It remained silent inside, and even the drips beside you had stopped, except for one, so small it didn't have the weight to free itself. You stood up and blood rushed to your head. Dizzy, you put your face close to the glass windowpane and squinted through to the dim kitchen. Vera sat very still and upright at the table, smoking. Her elbows were tucked tight to her side and her cigarette held at eye level. An unbroken blue line of smoke rose up like a puppet's string. It was so ordinary a thing, to sit at your kitchen table and have a smoke, that you thought you had got it all wrong.

Only then did you knock on the glass. Vera remained still. You knocked again and harder. She moved her hand just enough to allow the tip of her cigarette to touch her mouth. A slow billow of smoke.

You went to the back door and lifted the

latch, walking across the threshold to stand before her. Her cigarette had fallen and it lay smouldering into the kitchen table. Her eyes were hooded, and though still open she was so far behind them that nothing could be seen.

'Vera,' you say into the room. 'Vera,' you say again. The bowl in front of her was empty, the large glass of water too. You felt yourself suspended at the edge of the room. 'Can I help you?' you say. She blinked, two lazy blinks and her eyes rose up towards you.

'I . . . ' She stopped and one elbow skidded from under her, kicking out to the side, knocking the glass to the floor where it broke apart. She stood up then, swaying, and looked down at her hands, her fingers still holding the shape of the glass, and she says, 'Oh.' Just that. She looked at you, confused then frightened. Then her body started to collapse down, like when you jump into the sea, feet first, arms splayed to the side, waiting for the ocean to catch you.

She hit the floor with her eyes already closed, leaving you standing across from her with your hands empty and stretched into the room.

You could see the rise and fall of her chest but knelt down beside her and put your ear to her mouth until you felt her breath. You ran to the living room and gathered up a few pillows and rushed back to her, using them to lift her head off the cold floor.

'Vera,' you say, a whisper. 'Vera,' you say again. You looked along the line of her neck, her collarbone exposed, her white skin stretched over it.

A woman's voice asked the nature of your emergency and when you hesitated, she helped you along by suggesting, 'Gardaí or ambulance?'

'Ambulance,' you say and then added, 'please.'

After you'd given the address and hung up the telephone, you ran back from the hallway, down the three steps to the kitchen, and stood over Vera, unsure of what to do next.

Her breaths were shallow and her skin, when you put your hand to it, felt tacky and cool. She was dying. In the excitement it had never occurred to you. But she was trying to die, and she might have succeeded at any moment; her breath could just stop. Your hand could, just then, be across the forehead of something that was dead.

On the flagstones there were a few stray droplets of blood. A shard from the broken glass must have found its way inside her; you couldn't see where. You felt sick and a tear ran down your cheek. You were startled by it and rubbed your finger-tips along your face to check, even though you had clearly felt it on your skin, even though you'd have sworn that you had no feeling at all.

You heard the doorbell and ran to open it with an urgency the ambulance men refused to match. In a few moments they had her off the floor and hoisted like a rag doll onto the stretcher. One of them packed the empty tablet bottles. While strapping her in, they asked you questions. Was she allergic to anything? Her blood type? Her medical history?

'I don't know,' you say, so many times that finally you offered, 'Her name is Vera.'

'Yeah,' says one of them. 'I read that on the bottle.' But after that he must have taken pity on you, and before getting into the driver's side, he half smiled and says, 'She'll probably be all right.'

A few neighbours had come outside and stood by their steps, watching. The blue lights swept across their faces before moving on to Dun Laoghaire. Vera's front door was wide open. You went up the steps and closed it behind you.

In the kitchen you swept up the glass and brought the pillows back to the sitting room. You hesitated only a little after lifting the bowl off the table and seeing there were a few coloured tablets left. You wondered if they were evidence of some sort, but put them in the bin and washed the bowl regardless, leaving it to drain.

The patina had faded from the kitchen table: there were pockmarks blackened over the years. You found your nail moving in and out of one, leaving a mark. Vera's dropped cigarette had scorched an area. Only sandpaper and an afternoon's work would rid the table of it.

A book lay open where Vera had sat; she must have taken it from the small stack of books and read it while smoking and waiting for the tablets to work. Had it simply been at the top of the pile? Or were these the words she wanted in her head, her suicide note?

You made sure the lights were all out, and pulled the back door shut without locking it, then cleared the wall, taking the book with you.

14

You had never had a book before, and this one was a good one, you were sure of that, with its thumb-worn pages and old amber smell. The writer's name in bold red print, T. S. Eliot, and the simple word *Poems* across the top. On the cover, cutting through the word, was a perfect circle, a dark stain.

You saw her then, Vera, at home one night on that blue couch, a blanket over her knees, maybe a fire burning in the grate. She looped a strand of hair behind her ear and reached across and set a half-finished glass of red wine onto the book she had fully emptied. It left a mark.

You sat at the kitchen table and boldly put the book out in front of you. Your mother was making the dinner, the news on the radio. The boys were in the next room, the television too. When you came home your mother had resisted asking how much you had been paid, but she wanted to know; she was angry at you for making her ask.

'What's that?' she says.

'It's a book.'

'I can see it's a book, what book is it?'

'Poems,' you say.

'Poems?' She forced air through her pursed lips, making a kind of pap sound. 'What sort of poems?'

'Just poems.'

'Where did you get it?'

'From her.'

'Who?'

'Your woman I was working for.'

'She gave it?'

'Yes.'

'What's she doing, giving a book?'

'Don't know.'

'Of course you know. She gave it to you, didn't she?'

She came over and picked up the book, turning the pages over in her hand.

'What's her name?'

'Vera,' you say.

'Bloody Vera, Vera what?'

'Hatton, I think.'

'She's a Protestant so.'

'Don't know.'

'She can be what she wants as long as you're paid — did she pay you?'

'Yes, course.'

'How much? How much did she pay?'

'She's paying me next week.'

'I feckin' knew it. You thick, she didn't pay you. Tell the truth.'

'She's going to pay me next week . . . Give me back the book.'

She walked the book into the sitting room and held it out for your brothers to see.

'Look it,' she says. 'He does a day's work and she gives him a book.'

She came back to the kitchen but wouldn't surrender it. She flicked through its pages, searching.

'I'd like to know what she's doing giving books to young lads. Cheek of her, what age is she, I said what age?'

'I don't know.'

'Well, I do. She's laughing at you so she is, laughing her head off. Jesus Christ. A book.' She threw the book onto the table, and it slid across the surface, falling over the edge to the floor where it made a flat plop sound. The stain on the cover faced up; it was an ordinary stain, like the book was somehow broken and no longer special.

★   ★   ★

When your grandmother had died, before you were born, your mother, still young herself, had been told to go and claim something from her mother's house. When she got there, along with her own brothers, they had all walked slowly through the modest house. She

98

took hold of a large plant. A busy Lizzie. It was as much as she could carry.

Her brothers had been cute, had shown up with vehicles and stripped the home of its few antiques, right down to the window dressings. It wasn't much, but enough to fill a small lorry. Enough that years later, your mother would still remember, promising she'd never be made a fool of again.

You hated to let your mother see how you stooped to pick the book off the floor. That it was that important to you. But you had to stoop, so you did. You were determined.

You sat with the first page open, words written small enough that you could feel your eyes squint and your nose furl as you ran your finger along the sentences. There was the word '*love*', and it gave you hope. How awful it was for Vera, tossed about by strangers. You felt a new tear burn along your eyelid, and if you so much as blinked it would come, crashing down in a great drop across the table. Your mother would know you cared then, they all would. You stood and walked beyond the steam and the doom on the radio, out of the kitchen.

'By God, you didn't get far with that,' says your mother behind you. 'It's far from books now. Bloody books, come winter it's lumps of coal is all.'

Out past the living room and up the stairs. There was only the toilet, so you went in and locked the door behind you. You dropped to the floor and steadied your breathing. Slowly, slowly, you told yourself. It had hold of you. The bastard tears fell then, and you arched your head back until it hurt. In a sudden fit of rage you flung the book across the room; its old spine broke apart and loose pages fell in a shower. Slowly, slowly, red and black and yellow. Your mother was probably right; books were not for boys who cut meat.

15

Sharon was at Cats' Den, sitting on the rock like she was part of it.

'The head on you and the price of butter,' she says, careful not to seem surprised, but not expecting you either.

You sat down on the next dry rock. The boulder overhead served as a parasol for you both.

'You bunking school?' she asks.

You had hold of the book; you had taped its spine, but it was no use. The pages folded loose and uneven.

'Just a few classes,' you say. 'You got any smokes?'

'Yeah.'

'Giz one.'

'Fuck off.'

'Go on, I'll pay you back.'

She looked away from you, pretending you were not there, putting her nose in the air like she was posh. It was a game she played, and secretly you liked it.

'Don't be so tight,' you say. She was wearing jeans; you missed seeing her brown scratched legs and sometimes a flash of her pants.

'If I give you one, I want two back.'

'Go on then,' you say, holding out your hand. She opened her black bomber jacket, its orange lining showing as she took out a packet of twenty Player's.

'Where did you get them?'

'What are you, a bleeden' guard?' She handed you one.

'Did you buy twenty?'

'They were a prezzie,' she says.

'From who?'

She didn't answer. 'What's that?'

'Book,' you say, rocking it back and forth once before dropping it onto the wet ground and lighting your cigarette.

'Where did you get it?'

'The woman I'm working for.'

'Yeah?'

'Yeah.'

'Your girlfriend.'

'She's not my girlfriend.'

'Funny, the fella who bought me the smokes said the same thing.'

There was a pause, and old rain could be heard dripping unevenly from the branches and leaves of the trees. The smoke from your cigarette rose high into the damp air. You looked over to Sharon and saw then how she clenched and unclenched her fists.

'How come you're here so early?' you say.

'I was having a smoke in peace till you showed up.'

'You're delighted.'

'Am I fuck.'

'I'll say nothing.'

'Thanks.' She let her eyes rest on your face. 'Giz a look at that book.' When you picked it off the ground some wet muck and a single leaf had stuck to the back of it. You wiped it on your jeans and passed it.

'Did she not have a new one she could have given you?' She laughed at that, you both did, and then she fingered through the book undaunted, her mouth in time with the different words.

'Can you read that?' you say.

'Course I can read it. I couldn't tell you what he's shite'en' on about, but I can read it. Can you not?'

'I can read it, yeah,' you say.

'I always was good at the reading, I liked it, books and all,' she says, carefully. She was telling you a secret and secretly you saw how you were the same in that, even though you didn't want to be the same.

'Do you still?' You dropped your cigarette and it quickly extinguished.

'Nah.'

'Why not?'

'Just don't.'

'I don't know anyone that reads.'

Sharon flung the book back and it landed beside you. 'Not much use to you then, is it?' she says and shrugged and looked away. She started biting at her nails then, but caught herself and buried her hands deep in her pockets.

'Would you be my boyfriend?' she says, slow and cautious.

'What?' But you'd heard.

'I'm not asking you — I wouldn't touch you with a barge-pole. I'm saying would you? Would you be my boyfriend?'

You looked at her; she was nothing for that rock to hold. You saw then how you were seen in school and at the butcher's shop, even when Vera looked across at you and smiled kindly, asking you to do some work. And you, fool, had hoped.

'Yeah,' you say 'I would.' She smiled a bit, but you couldn't look for long.

'Do you want another smoke?' she says.

'Nah, I'm all right.'

She lit one, and rubbed her face before drawing on it.

'You ever visit someone up in St Michael's?' you say.

'Yeah, me grandad, years ago.'

'Hard to get in?'

'It's not a fucking nightclub.'

'Just asking.'

'Who's sick?'

'No one,' you say.

'Full of shite, you.' She drew on her smoke reluctantly, as if she was sorry she'd lit up so soon.

'Giz a drag,' you say. When she passed you the cigarette, the end was wet with her cold saliva, and it turned you on. When you thought of it with her, it was always rough and quick, animal, in need of relief and it didn't matter because you were loveless, you were flesh.

'You duck's-arsed it,' you say.

'If you don't want it give it back.'

Sharon stayed a while, but the chat died. You thought the silence unnerved her, but you couldn't be any other way then. She stood up, and before she made to go she insisted on leaving you with another one of her cigarettes. You picked the book up and cleaned it.

16

Missus O'Neill grew the best daffodils, everybody said so; as early as February they would begin to bloom in long yellow ribbons throughout her front garden. You ripped a handful from the muck, shedding wet soil from their bulbs. You'd been so frantic to get your hands on them that in your bouquet several were ruined. Gripping them tightly, you walked the coast road to the hospital. But before going inside, you threw them under a parked car and wiped your hands on your jeans.

You veered away from the reception area and lost yourself in the long corridors. At a nurses' station on the second floor, Vera's name was recognised and you were redirected to Recovery.

She was pale. Her eyes were closed and her lips tight and dry and you imagined her parched tongue sticking to the roof of her mouth.

Her bed was one of eight in the ward, two neat rows of four, Vera's furthest from the door. It was visiting hours, and the ward was busy with parents and children and balloons and orange-wrapped bottles of fizz. A chair was placed beside her bed; you were not the first to sit there.

You watched her, her body motionless save the rise and fall of her chest, the slight amount of air needed to sustain her.

You had brought the book to read to her, but even as you took it from your coat and leaned close with an open page, you were overcome with shyness. You had seen it in the films, loved ones reading quietly to loved ones, but all around you was chat and excitement and relief.

You took the first few lines of a poem, and said them in a whisper, a mumble. Slowly, word by word, like picking your way across wet rocks. Your eyes were moving from Vera to the book and back.

Her head rolled towards you; she pressed her eyelids tight and slowly opened them and took you in. You were a curiosity that she found slightly irritating.

'Stop,' she says, 'whatever you think you are doing, stop it.'

'It's T.S. Eliot.'

'I know who it is.'

'Isn't it your favourite?'

'No, it's not.'

'I thought . . . ' You found yourself looking at the book, and your banjaxed fingers draped across its spine.

'Who are you?' she says.

You wondered then, if really it might have been better to have given the book to Sharon, to encourage her to start reading again, seeing as how she had liked it. But what would be the point? Sharon never would and the bastard book was shit anyway.

'Sonny,' you say.

'Sonny?' The name meant nothing to her.

'From McCann's butcher's.'

'Sonny,' she says vaguely. 'I thought you were that young priest. Thank God.'

'It was me — I was the one who found you.' She looked at you then, really looked at you. Letting you know that she remembered you. That she would not be grateful for being found, that some part of her hated you.

A family arrived at the bed across from Vera. There were cries of 'Mammy!' and 'Be gentle now, your mammy is only getting better.' The mother sat up in bed, an adult helping to fix the pillows at her back. One of the men turned and smiled at Vera, his eye falling quickly across the shape her body made under the blankets.

'Help me up,' says Vera, and raised her elbow towards you.

'What?'

'Help me up, I'm going for a smoke.'

'Are you supposed to do that?'

'Do you think I care?' she says, and garnered a handful of disapproving looks from patients and visitors close enough to hear.

You stood up and when she put her hand on your shoulder to hoist herself off the high bed, you found your hand had shot up and rested on hers and as she slid off the bed part of her body brushed roughly against yours. Her feet found their way inside her slippers. She tightened her robe and walked ahead of you.

A nurse passed Vera in the long corridor and greeted her by name, stopping a moment to ask after her. 'Better now, Mary,' Vera says and, by way of a comfort, she touched her arm.

'I'm so glad,' says the nurse. 'All the girls upstairs were asking after you — they'll be delighted now, to hear you're up and about.' She looked at you then; you had stopped a few feet behind and waited, unsure. The nurse looked back at Vera to see if introductions were to be made; they were not.

The smoking room smelled like burning plastic. 'Do you want a cigarette?' Vera says, her own lit and a first puff of smoke already escaping her mouth. The packet felt big in your hands, American cigarettes, Camels.

You sat side by side on green plastic chairs

staring out the window, a perfect view of the wet car park. A faint slick of orange street light reflected back.

'Did you think to lock the door, after you left?' she says.

'Yes.'

'Good.'

'I cleaned up . . . a little.'

'Cleaned up?'

'Just some broken glass and the bowl and that.' You noticed then that her blue nightgown had been stamped *'St Michael's hospital'*; the same was true of her pyjamas and slippers, all supplied by the hospital. No one had come to visit.

'I painted the wall outside, the kitchen wall outside.'

'I can't pay you for it just now,' she says.

'No . . . That's not why . . . I just didn't want you surprised.'

'Surprised,' she says, rolling the tip of her ash onto the edge of an overflowing ashtray. 'Men have a much higher success rate than women, did you know that, Sonny?'

'Success?'

'With suicide.'

'No, I didn't.'

'Well, it's true, so much so that most people think that for women, it's a cry for help.'

She watched as an old man pushed open the heavy door. His slippers scraped on the polished floor as he passed them, then he sat down at the far end of the room and pointed a remote control at a TV bolted high up on the wall. The batteries must have gone: he pressed every button without bringing the small screen to life. He sat then, defeated, with the remote resting on his lap.

Vera turned to you, taking a last drag on her smoke and saying, 'I'm not crying for help, I don't want it. Do you understand?'

'Yes,' you say.

'Why did you bring that book?'

'It was on the table, open, when I found you.'

'You were outside, painting?'

'Yes.'

'Did you watch me?'

'Yes.'

'Through the window.'

'Yes.'

The old man began to shake the remote, pulling at its back, trying to remove the cover. His nails made a clicking sound.

'Aren't you supposed to leave a note?' you say.

'To whom?'

'I don't know.'

'Neither do I.'

'Is there no one?'

'Not like that,' she says. Her fingers began slowly tapping the top of her cigarette box. 'Why don't you go ahead and read me one of the poems — do you have a favourite?'

'No, I don't know them that well.'

She tut-tutted at that and told you to read the first one. The old man threw the remote down and stood and made his way to the door, saying, 'This place ... feckless gobshites.' Vera smiled then, and closed her eyes as you read.

A few poems later, you looked at her while pretending to flip the pages; her eyes were still closed but you didn't think she was sleeping. The palms of her hands rested flat on her lap, and under her robe you could make out her strong thighs. Eventually, she says, 'Thank you,' mostly under her breath.

Then she looked at a clock on the far wall and you saw how she had been waiting for visiting hours to end, so she could return to her ward, how it suited her just then to have you there.

'Bye now,' she says after you had held open the door and watched her walk through the long corridor. Her hands in her pockets, she never looked back.

17

On the walk home you told yourself you were just returning her book. You scaled the back wall and went in through the unlocked back door. It was late afternoon and although you wanted to stay longer, you were expected at the butcher's. You placed the book on top of the pile on the kitchen table, but you couldn't leave without taking another.

You stood in her front room, by the blue couch, holding on to the luxury of your boldness. Along her entire back wall, and left and right of her fireplace, were shelves of books. At first, you couldn't understand it, the books seemed littered, random. You saw then that she had placed them by country. The Irish, the English. Russian, French and the Americans. You picked a book, *Closely Observed Trains*. It was small enough that you could easily hide it.

That night, alone in the shed, you sat with some cardboard between you and the concrete floor, then wrapped yourself in two bath towels that had been waiting their turn by the washing machine. Only then, when you were settled, did you open the book.

You had hidden it first in your usual place

underneath the sink in the bathroom, and later you'd retrieved it and stuffed it down the front of your pants, covering its top with your jumper when you came down the stairs. You'd sat eating your dinner with it strapped to you like an incendiary device.

When you heard your father turning off the TV, you saw how long you had been out there and wondered if he was sorry you hadn't come and joined him. You wouldn't give the book up. When you were sure the house was sleeping you unwrapped yourself and went inside, made tea and stoked what was left of the fire. You took his chair and even lit a cigarette. It was slow going, but just before the sky hinted at light, you finished. And in closing the book you ran your hand over it, the way she might. The way she might come back from that silence, changed. You thought of her and all the rows of books she had, that feeling that she must have inside her, tenfold, a hundredfold.

★   ★   ★

'Have you been there all night?' says your mother, waking you, but it was too early for her to give much to it.

'No,' you say.

'Have you been smoking?' she says of the

ashtray sitting on the floor beside the chair.

'No, Da must have left it there.'

'Your father never leaves his ashtray there.'

'He did last night, why don't you ask him?'

She held on to you only a moment, her morning-tired eyes and face, before going into the kitchen where you heard her fill the kettle and turn it on. She was annoyed then and wouldn't offer you a cup.

You looked to the day ahead, the wet road to school, hiding in classrooms, listening in fear for your name to come, and it would come. The butcher's at four and the walk home. Your life was plain and small, you knew that for certain.

The book had slid between you and the chair's cushion. You tucked it back into your jeans and when you went to stand felt a dull pain all through your body. Upstairs, you went into the bathroom to hide the book, but then you didn't hide it.

You left your house with your canvas school bag dragging at your shoulder, having spent so long with the bathroom locked that your brother beat against the door.

★   ★   ★

It was only when your thumb pressed down on the cold steel of Vera's back-door latch

115

that it occurred to you: she might well have been released. It scared you, but not enough to stop you pushing the door open. You stood, studying the kitchen for hints of change, even though you imagined her living in the big house so lightly that it would be near impossible to tell.

You walked past the long table allowing your fingertips to drag along the wood. A lifeless smell was beginning to emerge. The house was excreting the first wafts of desertion.

You walked up the three steps to the hall, turning left into the sitting room, searching row upon row of books for the most thumb-worn of her collection. You weren't immediately worried for Vera, that she would try it again. Not yet. You knew that from home. It was like boiling a kettle; after you boiled it, you had to start again with cold water.

You returned the second book and searched for another. An area of her shelves was taken up with books about the National Gallery of Ireland. You found a small bronze plaque, thanking her for her service there.

You had never been to the National Gallery, though you knew where it was. There had been a school trip, a year earlier; you'd been excited, putting aside money for the bus fare. But then you learned there would be a lunch for the students in the gallery's café and it would have to be paid for, and anyway, you were sick that day.

Slowly you stood back from the shelves, holding a pile of books, then lay across the couch, pulling a blanket around you. Away from the dark morning and the wind through the ash and chestnut trees that lined up outside. The pelts of rain tap-tapping beyond the covered window. That room, a cold and silent sanctuary.

By mid-afternoon you were freezing, having only removed yourself from the couch a few times to piss. You saw how late it was, and taking *Silas Marner* with you, ran to the butcher's without first going home. That night, you again retreated to the shed and made your way slowly through its pages.

At midnight, your father became curious about what you were doing. It brought him out the kitchen door, and he looked down at you, wrapped in the towels with the open book on your lap. He held your eye for a second and then looked away.

'Don't let your mother see you with her towels,' he says, and closed the door.

★   ★   ★

'Have you come to read to me?' says Vera.

'If you like . . . If you have a book,' you say, the heavy door closing behind you. The lights were off in the smoking room and Vera was an L-shaped silhouette in a green chair, catching none of the creeping street light from the large window.

You had walked, first past her empty house, too frightened to go inside, then continuing along the road until you'd reached the hospital. You'd waited outside, watching through the plate glass for the matron to move away from her post, then you'd gone along the dim corridor and up the stairs, passing occasional late-night visitors coming to and from the intensive care unit, murmurs of difficult conversations echoing off the sterile walls and floors. From the doorway of her ward, you had seen that Vera's unmade bed was empty, the sheets and pink blanket in a great mound at its base.

'I couldn't sleep,' you say and walked over and sat down next to her.

'Are you here to see me or is there someone else you're visiting?'

'You, I'm here to see you.'

'What would you have done if I was asleep?'

'Don't know, waited . . . woken you.'

She smiled and passed you the packet of

smokes she held in her hand.

'Do you know what I'd love . . . ' she says. 'Toast, with real butter and marmalade. Decent fucking coffee.' She had not put her slippers on and her big toe closest to you had a scrape of red nail varnish.

'There is a farter in my ward. I've not located her, but she's there . . . farting.'

You laughed and she seemed to like that.

'There's another woman, about my age, she has these awful little snot-nosed children that pile around her every day. I don't think she's sick, she's on sabbatical. When they leave, she takes out a magazine and visibly relaxes.'

'Have you children?' you say, but she didn't like that. A long ash toppled from the end of her cigarette and fell unnoticed.

'Are your feet cold?' you say.

'No. What's your story, Sonny?'

'Don't know.'

'Have you a crush on me or something?'

You looked away and felt your face flush.

'No need to be coquettish about it.'

'I don't know what that means.'

'It means you need to read more. Not too old for you, no?' She looked at you then and you were brave and held her stare.

'No,' you say.

'I suppose if that's what works for you.

119

What's with the wine, the red wine, who is that for?'

'Me.'

'Just you?'

'Yeah.'

'Bit flowery for your neck of the woods, no?'

'My neck of the woods?'

'Look, if you are going to pretend to be stupid, I'm going to find another friend. Yes, your neck of the woods, the end where teenage lads don't drink red wine.' As she lit another cigarette, the small flame illuminated her face. You watched her hands fold around the flame and her mouth press forward.

'Why did you move to Ireland?'

'I like the rain.'

'You must fucking love it.'

'Who cares, Sonny. I mean, really? It's a story.'

'I do,' you say.

'Well, good, you make one up and we'll both believe it.'

You were lost then, you really had no idea how to speak with her. If it were Sharon, you'd just have pushed her, and she'd have pushed you back and that would be that. But you sat in the dark room, in the silence, and smoked. You were glad to know you had the duration of time a fresh-lit smoke gave you, each puff falling like pink sand from an hourglass. The silence between you was enough. You watched her, secretly at first, then allowed your stare to openly settle here and there, as you pleased, and she showed no signs of discomfort. She was beautiful, your Vera. And perhaps was used to being watched.

She turned then, and caught your eye on purpose, held it like a vice, like an inspection. Your eyes and nose and mouth and chin.

'You're too young to be lonely. Where are your friends?' she says.

'Where are yours?'

She continued to watch you and might have said something, but her attention was turned to the sound of quick footsteps from the corridor. They stopped and at once the door was pushed open.

'Oh, it's you in here, Vera,' says a nurse, scarcely filling the door frame. You could see a dark crucifix, strapped to the wall behind her. It frightened you; the crucifix had always frightened you.

'Yes,' says Vera. 'My nephew has paid a visit, from Wexford.'

'Oh, well,' says the nurse.

'We're not disturbing you?'

'It's certainly bending the rules, as you know. I mean, really, he should not be let up

121

at this late hour. It might make the other women uncomfortable.'

'Of course,' says Vera.

'Right so.' The nurse nodded sharply once and the door closed behind her.

'That's your marching orders, I think,' she says.

'What's she got against people from Wexford?' you say, standing. She smiled a bit and you wondered if you were making it up because you wanted it to be true, or did she seem disappointed that you were leaving?

'Thanks for the visit,' she says.

'Yeah,' you say, standing over her. She looked up with a slight smile.

'You'd better go before you make the women uncomfortable.'

18

In your school bag you had twelve and a half grammes of fresh tobacco and some rolling papers. You skinned up and passed Sharon the tobacco.

'You hopping off?'

'Yeah, going in to the National Gallery.'

'Where?'

'National Gallery, in town. Where they keep all the pictures.'

'Pictures of what?'

'Paintings.'

She lit her smoke, and her eyes searched the ground.

'Yeah . . . but what for?'

'Jaysus, I don't know, 'cause it's there, suppose . . . It's not here. I've never been, have you?'

'No, I haven't. And I'm not going to either.'

'Why not?'

'Just not.'

'That woman I was working for used to work there.'

'Why don't you marry her?'

'Do you not want to come, on the bus with me?'

'Nah.'

'I'll spot you.'

'Nah, it's not that, just don't want to go.'

You sat smoking, two, maybe three more smokes. Passing the tobacco between you both. You knew her feelings were hurt somehow and it was your fault, but you couldn't explain it. When you stood to leave you took a handful of tobacco from the pouch and passed it to her with some papers. You could see she thought about not taking them and you were glad when she did, as though she had forgiven you for leaving her there.

'See ya,' you say.

'Where is it?'

'What, the gallery?'

'Yeah.'

'It's in town.'

'I know that, where?'

'Off Merrion Square.'

'Just wondering,' she says, and then just before you were gone, she says, 'Thanks for asking me, an' all.'

★　★　★

The bus stop at Temple Hill was crowded with old ones, tightly holding their tartan wheelie bags, their pensions hidden for a day out in town. They came along slowly, one by one, breathless, and the others would all turn and by way of a hello say something about the weather, just to make them feel welcome. They were frail and held to kindness as a last defence.

You thought it must be nice to have a granny or grandpa. Yours were dead and you didn't know to miss them.

It took a long time for them to step onto the bus when it did come. The driver was young and impatient; he accelerated and stopped quickly, that was his style. His passengers were forced forward and then back into their seats, past Booterstown and the line stretching around the American embassy. The old ones shared silent looks of fear and disappointment.

Once you were outside, planted on the path, the air felt good and full of puff. You were distracted by the crowds, the white sky and the rush of bodies. You'd forgotten yourself enough to miss your turn and rather than admit the fault and stop and turn back, you continued around Merrion Square the long way, right on Lower Fitzwilliam Street, and then right again until you'd come fully around the park and found it.

It was a grand building. Probably Portland stone, you thought. It pleased you, telling yourself, as if you knew. It was something you had heard your dad say a long time ago. The Brits liked to build all their big buildings with Portland stone, but you didn't know how he could know that without someone telling him. And who would tell him?

The building scared you. They built them like that, the grand steps, the columns, the clean lines. You got that look from the security guard just inside the door; he recognised you as one of his own. It was free in, but you didn't trust it.

You went left, away from the reception through a wide lit corridor, and were steadying yourself to be told you were not allowed in, steadying yourself to seem as if, really, you didn't care. But no one came, and you were inside a room, big like a church, huge paintings hung inside gilded frames. Two oak stairs at the end inviting you deeper inside. You felt safe then, you were not sure why, but your hands came out of your pockets and weren't trembling. No one was watching. You had the hulking room to yourself and even as you craned your head you couldn't see all the ceiling at once, your own footsteps creaking and pushing against the old wood floor.

You could see her, Vera, as clear as if she'd just come in, unbuttoning her mac as she walked, maybe removing her gloves, pulling one finger free at a time, fixing her hair from where the wind had blown it across her reddened cheeks, and saying a quick hello to passing staff.

You went through the rooms slowly, but soon the big wars and wigged English and Spanish heads became dull enough that by the second or third room you were slowly admitting to yourself that you were bored and wondering about a cup of tea and a smoke. Then you found a Spanish monk; he was starving and in agony and it held you. You read what was said beside each painting but then made up your own story, building it to fit the shape of every frame.

An older couple stood whispering in front of a painting like they knew something and you were feeling just brave enough to stand close by and listen, stepping quietly as if your eye had been drawn in the same direction. You listened, but all you heard was a sudden burst of Sharon Burke's hoarse call, echoing through the room.

'Fuck sake, Sonny. Your da would be scarlet if he saw you.'

The old couple turned in disbelief. The woman reached for her partner's arm, pulling on it, directing him away.

Sharon walked towards you, a packet of cheese-and-onion crisps crinkling in her hand. Close behind her trailed the security guard. Stepping beside you then, she says, 'Don't mention anything, but I think John-Jo here fancies me.' And she looked over her shoulder at the guard and took to laugh.

'Shut up the fuck,' you say. 'You'll get us both thrown out.' She was unsure then, and whatever it was she had built up in herself was suddenly gone. She looked away from you, up the walls to the pictures, and reached in and found a crisp.

'Jaysus,' she says, 'you don't have to be a bollox about it. I spent twenty-five pence on the bus fare.'

You noticed then, she had make-up on her face, and she was wearing a white cotton dress under her bomber jacket. She had gone home and changed her clothes, and she had done it for you; it left a dull sickness in your chest and you thought to say something nice, but you couldn't and she felt that and says, 'I knew they'd be stupid fucking pictures, I knew I shouldn't have come in here.'

Just then, the security guard came closer. 'You can't eat them in here,' he says.

'Ah, ask me fanny,' says Sharon. You grabbed the crisps out of Sharon's hand and took hold of her, swinging her around and marching away from the guard.

'It's all right,' you say, but he followed anyway.

In the next room, Sharon says, 'What are you supposed to do here?'

'I don't know, look at the pictures.'

'I already looked at them.'

'Look at them again.'

'Why, have they changed?'

'Shut up.'

'Come on, Sonny, this is boring, I want to leave.'

'Well, go on then.'

'Come with me, fuck's sake, I come all this way.'

You were about to tell her you didn't want to, that you wanted to stay, but just then you heard the guard, who had been hovering: 'That's it now, any more language from you and you're out.'

You looked for an exit sign and were already reaching across for Sharon when something else had hold of you, and you faced the guard as he stood there, secure in his blue uniform, his tightly fitted cap perfectly aloft his head, his dark visor drawing a shadow under his eyes.

'What have you against her?' you say.

'Don't be smart with me, you pup. She's breaking the rules here. Now out, the pair of you.'

'I'm not being smart, I'm asking you, what you have against her. 'Cause you've been following her since she come in. You made up your mind about her as soon as you saw her.'

'Out,' he says, unclipping his walkie-talkie from his belt and clicking it to life.

'She hasn't been here before — how is she to know your rules? You could just tell her nice instead of creeping after her like a cunt, hoping to catch her out.'

Your mouth had gone dry then and your words were sticking.

'Come on,' says Sharon, 'we'll just go.' Her face was full of fright, her narrow shoulders collapsing. You walked towards the exit, stopping then, remembering.

'I need to go to the gift shop,' you say to Sharon. You turned back to the guard and shouted, 'I'm going to the gift shop now, you can follow me there if you want.' He did, him and the second guard that had joined him. They stood close by you and Sharon as you queued silently and paid for the book, with people looking on.

★ ★ ★

Outside, Sharon screamed, 'That was fucking brilliant.' She lit a smoke and screamed again, smoke pouring from her nose. 'Brilliant.'

You glanced back at the two guards standing high on the steps, a massive column on either side of them.

You were quiet on the bus home. Near your stop, Sharon says, 'We should do something, something different. I'm too buzzed to go home.'

The bus was mostly empty. You had sat upstairs and just then, to your left, as the bus held at a red light, you could see clearly inside a café. An old man sat alone behind a steaming plate of chips, looking out the window at the traffic, and you were sitting there, looking at him.

'I'm not getting off this stop,' you say to Sharon.

'Why not?' she says, and you could feel her studying your face.

'I'm just not, I'm getting off the next stop.'

'Are you going to that woman's?'

'Yeah.'

'Is that who the book's for?'

'Yeah.'

'I'll come with you.'

'Nah, you're all right.'

'I will, I'll come.'

'I don't want you to.'

She stood up, just as the bus rolled over a pothole, and it knocked her forward a little; she steadied herself and pushed past you. Your knees touched just below her lovely dress. And after she had gone, and the bus

131

rumbled forward, you were left to wish you had mentioned, just once, how she looked nice.

19

You rang Vera's doorbell, but mostly out of caution. Already you knew she wasn't there, making you brave enough to press the button hard, recklessly sending the tin noise through the house. When it stopped, the silence thickened inside. You stepped back from her door, turning on the step and looking out. It would stay bright for another twenty minutes, no more than a half-hour, that was certain.

You took out the book of pictures you had bought, still in that nice paper bag they gave you with the gallery name on it. A number of the paintings inside the book you had just seen in person and it made you feel you knew something. It was four pounds and twenty-five pence. You had taken ten pounds from your hiding place, used one ninety on the pouch of tobacco that you had shared with Sharon, plus twelve pence for the skins. There was the bus fare too.

It was the first book you had ever bought. It was yours, you could bring it home and hide it and any time you wanted to see it, you could just lock the bathroom door and feel for it. Later, when Vera was dead, and the book was just a book, the pictures would still move you.

There was a single bird sitting on a bare ash branch, unmoving, a black statue, and from your raised position on the step you could get a clear sense of its size: huge, like in a cartoon, huge.

You thought about visiting Vera at the hospital and sharing your discovery with her, but it had started to rain and anyway you'd lost your nerve. The back door was open, you knew that, you knew how it was to slip inside her house and in, out of the rain.

You walked through the side lane, checking the neighbour's upstairs window before clearing the back wall and running down the wet path to the door. You knew the kitchen well now, the way you learn a person's face.

Up the little steps to the hallway; the faintest strip of green light shone through the stained glass above the hall door and spread out in tiny shapes along the wall. You stood and watched, knowing the colour would disappear. How often Vera must have stood, the dark evening coming, and felt dread.

It made you sad to think of her there by herself.

Until then you had resisted going back to her bedroom, confining yourself to the kitchen and living room, but her unmade bed drew you back, the smell like deep sleep, the books on the floor, clothes carelessly strewn about: more of her here than in any other room in the house, and that made it your favourite room. There was some dark fabric under her pillow, and when you picked it up it felt soft and slid easily through your hands. You held it over the light, and it unfurled into a slip, a mould of her body.

When you sat down on the side of the bed, the springs gave a little, but not much. You looked around and recognised that this room was her secret, that you shouldn't have been there. Not that it was wrong, no, not that, but something more. You could feel it without having the words to say it, a type of sorry. Not the sorry from robbing or getting hit or chased or even the sorry when you'd find your ma in a state or when your brothers jeered at your da behind his back. It was a new sorry that you felt you'd have for always.

The doorbell rang then, a thick and violent sound that echoed through the house, leaving a ringing in your ears long after it stopped. You looked desperately around the room for anything you had touched or moved. The doorbell rang again, bringing you to your feet this time. You crept out of the room and across the upstairs landing, and stood breathless looking down at the front door. You could hear footsteps on the other side, then a sudden banging on the wood.

You were sure it was the guards. A neighbour must have seen you scale the back wall and called them. You descended the stairs, silently, inching towards the back door, though you already imagined the dark shape of a guard posted there, waiting.

'Sonny, fuck's sake, it's pissing.' You ran to the front door and found a rain-soaked Sharon standing there.

'Fuck you doing?'

'Ah, shut up the fuck, I'm soaking,' she says and tried to push past you.

'You can't come in.'

'Outta me way,' she says, a wet foot already planted on the step, and drips of rain coming off her white hair. She stood in the hall, the back of her coat leaving a streak of wet on the wall behind her.

'Close the fucking door, I'm freezing.'

'You can't be here.'

'Why not?'

'Cause you just fucking can't.'

'What are you doing here?'

But you don't answer that. Sharon smiled a bit.

'Are you working for your posh friend? Here, missus? Hey, missus?' Her voice rose through the empty house. 'I'd like to meet her, she sounds fucking great.'

'She's not here.'

'No?'

'I'm minding the place — she asked me to mind it.'

'Did she?'

'Yeah, she did.'

'Did she not give you any keys?'

'Wha'?'

'Keys, did she not give you keys? Is that why I saw you going over the wall? Now close the fucking door and stop being a prick.'

She pushed past you, turning into the living room, and you followed.

'Don't sit there, you'll get the couch all wet.'

Her make-up in streaks, she let her wet bomber jacket slip from her shoulders and land on the floor. 'Jaysus, Sonny. Look at you, you're fucking pathetic, running around like a mammy.'

'What do you want? I already told you to fuck off.'

'Where is she, Sonny?'

'None of your business.'

Sharon walked to the bookshelf; her hand moved across the spines of the books.

'You could be done for this. Six months, breaking and entering. They'd love a pretty boy like you in the Joy.' She pulled a random book from the shelf and flung it towards you. It caught your neck and it hurt.

'You read that one?' she says.

'Don't do that.'

She picked up another and flung it.

'You read that one?'

'Please,' you say. Your voice made this awful sound, where some feeling you didn't know you had flared like a lit match. It changed something in her, she looked down at the third book in her hand, and slowly returned it to the shelf.

'You were good to me today, weren't you, Sonny? Defending me and all.'

'Suppose,' you say. Through her pale wet dress, you could see a perfect outline of her body.

'You think you know her, 'cause you're here, but you don't,' she says.

'I know I don't.' You saw what Sharon saw, so clear it cut through you. But you knew what you felt, and that was right too.

'It's a bit weird, isn't it? You bein' here and all?'

'Suppose.'

'Where's her telly?'

'Doesn't have one.'

'Stupid cow.' She looked up to the ceiling, the eroded uneven mouldings high above her. 'This all hers?'

'Yeah, think so.'

'One person?'

'Yeah.'

'Jaysus.' Sharon left the room then, and her runners made a squelching sound where the rain had found its way in through a hole. She walked down the steps to the kitchen and stood there breathless, pushing her hair from her face.

'Jaysus,' she says again. She looked at you once, just because you were there and she had remembered. You saw her serious face, her mouth moving slowly trying to know something; her eye piercing the far corners of the room.

You saw the back of her neck when she passed you again. Where her hair stopped, the back of her dress had been stained by rain, the white changed to a blue-grey stretching down like a map of somewhere unknown.

In the hallway, she looked up the stairs and put a foot there, on the first step, the muscles of her thigh tightening. She cautiously put her fingers on the rail, not quite trusting at first. You didn't want her going upstairs, but let her without protest. Watching her body, how it moved, step by step, you admitted to yourself how it was a lonely business to break into someone's home and that you were glad to have Sharon's company. She paused at the upstairs balcony, crossed the hall and cautiously pushed open three of the four doors to empty bedrooms, their bare floorboards brushed clean. At Vera's bedroom she held the door open with one outstretched arm and stood still. And even though you didn't say, 'Don't go in there,' you felt she recognised the same thing you recognised, the same secret, and pulled the door shut without protest.

After Sharon had satisfied something by walking through the house, you sat, side by side on the rug, with your backs pressed into the blue couch.

'I don't understand it,' she says. 'You, I don't understand you. You're going to get into trouble, you know that?' You looked along her cold legs, down her thighs and calves. Her arms were crossed and pulled self-consciously in to her belly. You reached back and took up Sharon's coat, still damp, and spread it over you both.

'Where is she?'

'Hospital.'

'What's wrong with her?'

'Don't know.'

'Are you sleeping in her bed?'

'No.'

'I'd fucking kill you if you did that.'

You were suddenly tired and let your head fall forward and land on your knees. You thought to reach out and touch her bare legs.

'You think you're better than me, don't you?' she says. 'You want to be better than everyone, don't you? A snob, aren't you?' But you didn't think you were better than Sharon, you were the same as Sharon, you were Sharon.

The rain seemed to have stopped and the wind died back as the afternoon darkened. The cold house surrounded you both; you closed your eyes. At your arm and shoulder you could feel the heat from Sharon, she pushed into you, searching for that same warmth. If you were different, generous, you would have wrapped your arms around her and pulled her towards you, finding comfort for you both. Instead you both drifted with prickles of cold air around you and even when Sharon reached over and covered your hand with hers and tightly held your index finger in her fist, you did not respond.

★ ★ ★

When you woke it was perfectly dark and your neck hurt and you could feel the weight of Sharon's body beside you. Her slow and even breathing. It felt late and you were confused. You could clearly hear the sound of

141

a key turning in a lock, it was what had woken you. Then you heard the front door open and slam shut with authority. A bright overhead light blazed through the room and you saw Vera, standing in a wet mac holding a thin plastic bag with some shopping. Later, you'd remember seeing a bottle of milk and some butter. A packet of Bourbon creams. But no bread; she had forgotten the bread and would be hungry later, looking at the butter with the shops all closed.

'Oh, Christ,' says Vera. She stepped back with fright. You stood up. Sharon was looking around as confused as you had been.

'It's Sonny, it's OK, it's me, it's just Sonny.'

'Oh, fuck, fuck, fuck,' says Vera in these quick exhales, fighting for her breath. She had first held her free hand to her mouth and then doubled over her shopping. She was breathing hard, you thought she might be sick. Sharon stood then; her skirt had rolled up her leg while she slept and she was pulling it down towards her knees. She looked so ragged that you were embarrassed for her, embarrassed for you both.

'What are you doing? What are you doing in my fucking house?'

'We weren't . . . nothing,' you say.

'Out. Get out,' says Vera, screaming. Her hair fell forward, covering some of her face.

She looked tired, drained, as if some of the hospital had clung to her as she travelled home by the Monkstown Road.

'Me coat,' says Sharon, searching under the coffee table. She pulled it from the floor and walked quickly around Vera with her head lowered and out the door. 'Sorry, missus,' she says.

Alone then, Vera looked up at you. It focused all your attention towards her face, and you saw that her eyelashes were wet; you couldn't see the tear, and you wondered if, when your back was turned from her, she had slyly wiped it with her hand.

'Out,' she says, softer then.

'We weren't . . . I'm sorry' you say.

'If I ever see you anywhere near this house again I'll call the police.' She collected herself, and her voice seemed strange to you.

'The police?' you say, and you could feel your face scrunch up into a question.

'Yes, the fucking police. You've frightened me,' she says.

'Yes,' you say.

'Just get out of my sight.'

You held on for as long as you could and then walked past her, out into the dark hallway. You could see Sharon waiting at a safe distance from the house. You pulled the door shut and began to walk with Sharon at your side. She was talking but you couldn't make sense of it, because just then, you were so filled with hatred for her.

20

In the cold room at the back of the butcher shop, the split beef carcasses swung on old hooks. Sometimes when no one could see, you punched the soft bit under the ribs, your hand bloodied with wet slaps, but it was not your blood, and afterwards you could just wash it off.

Vera wanted to die, but if you could bring her here, into the cold room with the cold swinging dead things that meant nothing and could be punched and eaten and their blood washed away without a second thought, then she would see what dead was and not want it. You were the hero in your dream of saving her, even with everything you didn't know about her.

You had thought often of saving your mother, but saw how you had given up being her hero.

★　★　★

'Sonny you'll be late now, get up,' your mother called from the bottom of the stairs. You lay still, a blanket wrapped tight around

145

you, eyes open. The curtains were drawn but were too thin to stop the light passing through. Your clothes were in a heap on the floor beside you; last night you had discarded them as if you would never need them again. You swung your legs out from the lower bunk bed and the cold air found you. When you pushed into your jeans they felt damp, and your jumper held old sweat and tobacco.

'I'm next,' says a brother, standing outside the locked bathroom door. So you went downstairs needing a piss. Your father sat at the kitchen table, a mostly eaten bowl of cornflakes in front of him with a few hardened flakes around the rim and a small bit of milk that he couldn't get to with the spoon. He smeared a slice of white bread with butter and dipped his cornflake spoon into the packet of sugar; white granules danced across the table as he spilt the sugar over the bread, folding it in two before he started roughly chewing. Your mother stood at the sink, and through her eyes you felt disgust.

'Where are your brothers?' she says and walked past you, her voice calling at the base of the stairs. But you knew they were hiding up there until he was finished. Your mother knew it, and surely he must've known it too.

You put the kettle on and stood with your

hand on the steel draining board, feeling the vibrations of the slow boiling. Through the window, the small neglected back garden moved patiently through spring; the grass had risen and the old rockery in front of the big wall was overgrown. There was a laburnum tree that used to grow in the middle of the garden, and by this late in the season you'd expect to see the first scatter of buds that would become a million yellow blossoms. Your mother had grown afraid of it, saying it was too big, its roots would grow under the house and upend the foundation. You had felt proud and capable when she had sent you out one Sunday morning last summer to hack at its lower branches and upper branches and kill it down to its roots, until the generous little laburnum lay in folds across the grass. By the afternoon the hot sun had taken the tree's colours from yellow to brown to no colour at all, and even your mother's blessing was not enough to sanctify it.

The kettle clicked, and your father stood in his socks and lumbered out of the kitchen. They would come down then, careful not to pass him on the stairs. In his absence there was the first flicker of small conversation. The table was destroyed, his uneaten crusts sucking up the milk in his bowl. Your mother would clean it up, tut-tutting at the state of it.

You heard the bathroom door open and close. You looked at the clock and saw you'd not get the time to piss before you would have to leave, so you walked out the back door, through the shed, and quickly pissed outside at the coal bunker. A hot yellow stream that delighted you.

The housing estate seemed empty as you walked through it, holding the worn and jagged strap of your school bag away from your neck. In the lane you set the bag down and checked both ways for anyone coming and lit a cigarette. You carefully exhaled through your nose and played the game where Vera watched you, admiring you as you stood, one leg forward and the other back, the sole of your shoe pressed against the wall. You wondered if she was home and for a moment you considered going and standing in front of her house where maybe she'd see you from her window and a few moments later she'd come to her door. But you were too afraid to see her; that was the truth.

You pulled so hard on the cigarette that it made you light-headed and sick enough to stub it half smoked against the wall, dropping the butt end in your pocket, which later you regretted because your whole coat was rank with it.

Your first class was maths. You liked Miss

Harris; she was a soft woman with small gold glasses that had a jewelled string hanging arm to arm, and sometimes when she was tired she took the glasses off, and there they hung around her neck like a curious medallion. When you came into her classroom she was standing with her back to the room, stretched on her toes and writing numbers across the blackboard.

When Miss Harris talked about maths she became excited, though she had learned to hide it, and you decided that when she was young she was teased.

Miss Harris was kind to you. They weren't all like her; some of them secretly wanted to be liked, and right when you thought they would leave you be, they stood at the top of the class and said your name until everyone turned to face you. They'd found the runt of the litter and slowly they would starve it out.

Some sun must have broken through the blanket of cloud because dropping between your desk and the floor was a lovely streak of sunlight. Your eyes became heavy, and when you closed them there was warmth, pink and red, coupled with the rise and fall of Miss Harris's posh voice, and it reminded you of Vera and helped you forget what you'd done to not have her.

It was then that the loudspeaker crackled to

life and went silent and came back to life again. 'Sonny Knolls, please come to the principal's office immediately, that's Sonny Knolls to the principal's office.' You were looking at the speaker then; it ceased to have any life so quickly that you had to look around at your classmates to see if they had heard it too. Your hands had started to tremble. Miss Harris pushed her glasses further up her nose and rolled a piece of white chalk like a cigarette between her thumb and forefinger.

'Collect your things, Sonny, and go on up,' she says in a serious, almost worried way, and for an instant you thought you should really try harder in her classroom.

You left the room and made your way, putting on your coat as you went down the bare wooden stairs, leaving behind you the murmur of lessons.

Outside, the light burned, but it was not warm, not warm enough that it lifted the wet from the shining tarmac that ran like the strait of a river between the old red-brick building and the newer single-storey that made up the bulk of the school. Students were buttoned into their classes, and the road was clear; the school seemed empty and not real.

21

The door to the principal's office, half-filled with safety glass, was slightly ajar but still you knocked. A woman's disinterested voice called you in. You saw the secretary sitting behind an old wooden desk and she pointed her arm towards a row of benches. When you looked back a moment later her attention had returned to her work.

Time stood still and there was only the sound of her pen pulling across the page. Then you heard footsteps in the corridor outside, and the door was pushed open, and in the doorway was the red-haired prefect who had chased you. You had dreaded seeing him since that day, so much so that he'd come to your dreams twice, but now you were surprised to discover how ordinary a thing it was for him to stand across from you, looking down with his clean and knowing face.

'Thanks for coming, Graeme,' says the secretary. 'Just take a seat, he won't be long.'

'That's fine, fine,' he says and sat not far from you along the bench. He seemed so mature and capable beside you, even though he could not have been more than a year older. You wondered how he'd done it. How, in almost the same number of years as you, had he gone that far? You watched him; he'd hardly registered that you were there, but he didn't ignore you enough that it meant anything. It was more the way you would be with a piece of furniture. He was comfortable and filling the bench with his knees wide apart, the way boys do if they want you to think that they have big balls.

'You'll be a while getting through that lot,' he says of the large pile of papers on the secretary's desk.

She arched her back a little and chuckled before turning to him with a wide smile.

'Oh, indeed I will,' she says and covered her poorly fitted teeth with her hand. 'Indeed.' She looked away and collected herself, embarrassed at giving too much. 'You sent Blackrock home with very little, Saturday,' she says, without looking over.

'They brought very little,' says Graeme, and the two of them took to laugh.

'You played it well, very well,' she says in such a shy and kind way that you couldn't help but like her.

'A good game all right. Few more of them till we see the final, that would be all right.'

Graeme settled back into his own satisfied

thoughts, until the principal's door opened and he immediately stood and greeted Principal Burke with a firm handshake as he emerged from his office. You thought to stand also, but found you could not.

'Graeme,' says Principal Burke. 'Thanks for taking time on all this . . . time-wasting nonsense. This, this little thieving . . . I don't know what you'd call him, I know what I'd like to call him. Fecker that he is. What I want you to do is just go through the details when he gets here, if that's all right with you. Now, if it's too, I don't know, embarrassing for you, we can find another way.'

'Not at all,' says Graeme. 'Happy to do it — he's here.'

He turned to indicate where you were sitting on the bench. Principal Burke's face hardened as if he was looking at something awful. There was a theatricality to it that made you suspect him, as if he had known you were there all along and had wanted you to hear him call you a thieving fecker.

'Inside, you,' says the principal and he walked ahead. Graeme had stopped before the doorway, waiting, so you would have to pass him before going in, and even though you promised yourself you wouldn't catch his eye, you did. He smiled at you and mouthed the words, You're dead.

Principal Burke took his position behind the desk; he was a big man and frustrated with his own lumbering movement. It seemed a private thing, so you did not look up at him until he was finished sitting.

'Open or closed, Principal Burke?'

'I think open is fine, leave in some air.'

Graeme came through the room, and you could feel the whoosh of him passing before he took a seat in one of two plain wooden chairs set in front of Principal Burke's desk.

'Mr Knolls? Would you care to join us?' says Principal Burke, his eyes drifting over you once and then blinking tight.

'OK, Graeme, if you would, a quick account of the events.' He turned to check the clock above a large bookcase. On the bookcase, behind lovely bevelled glass, was a row of thick red books.

'Following a discussion among the prefects about the spate of bike vandalism, it was decided that we would take turns to keep a watch from behind the tuck shop to see if we could catch the vandal in the act. On the morning of the twenty-third I took up position . . . ' He had it rehearsed. It was perfect, and you could see Graeme now, between brushing his teeth and spitting, his eyes on himself in the mirror, going over his lines, looking this way and that until he had it. His words went into the room like a picture, spreading all around you in gradual strokes. He had a nice voice, Graeme, you thought and looked back over at the bookshelf. It was not mahogany, but oak that had been dark stained and made to look like mahogany. That's what they did in the olden days, a fella that worked alongside you and your father had told you once, and you agreed with him when he said it made no sense, that oak was too lovely a wood to be dressed up as something else. The red books had gold roman numerals on them, and you thought you'd never know how to stack them in the right order and wondered if Principal Burke had stacked them himself, back when he had first got the job. Standing on a chair with his young secretary fussing around him until he grew impatient and insisted on doing it himself.

Principal Burke took on the demeanour of a priest or judge, sitting back with his hands clamped tightly together across his belly, his chin resting on his chest. It suited him.

You wished you'd made it into the bathroom that morning; after pissing you might have thought to wash your hands with soap and that pink nailbrush. And then you wouldn't have had to sit here with your hands hidden between the top of the chair and your thighs and your dirty fingers starting to sweat.

Graeme never drifted from the truth: you'd done everything he said you'd done, more times than they knew. You were the little thief in his story. But still you felt that it was wrong, and that what they were doing to you was worse than your stealing. Graeme, sitting there showing off to Principal Burke, and Principal Burke who had already made up his mind about you and what he was going to do to you and then leaving the door open, where anybody passing could just hear all the bad things you'd done.

'Do you have anything to say?' You looked up at Principal Burke and saw that it was not the first time he'd asked you. You were shocked by his face. There was no feeling in it; when he looked at you there was nothing. It was a violent nothing that made you catch your breath. You didn't have the hardness where things could wash over you and you could just laugh the way you'd seen people laugh. And you felt that awful flush, and all you could produce was a hot drip at the base of your eye and the start of a tear.

'I didn't,' you say, and that was all, because you could see the reason now why you were here. They wanted to see what pieces had come together to make you up. The principal's expression had changed, there was

156

some knowledge that he was glad about; you had confirmed something that he'd suspected all along. He put his hand on the table, opening a red folder.

'Oh, I think you did, Mr Knolls,' he says. 'Thank you, Graeme. That will be all.'

You could feel Graeme's body standing beside you, but before he went, he leaned across Principal Burke's desk asking, 'May I?'

You didn't look up to see the exchange, but a moment later you saw the white of a tissue thrust under your nose. You had no choice but to take it between your fingers and look at him. He was clever, and in front of Principal Burke he gave nothing away. You held the tissue but didn't wipe your tears with it, and you thought that that was a very timid victory, as you heard Graeme give the secretary a friendly goodbye.

'Good luck on Saturday,' she says.

Principal Burke sat back in his chair and pushed his fingers into his chin. He said nothing until after he had opened a drawer in his desk and taken out a piece of paper with the school's letterhead printed on top in bold important letters. He moved it left and right across the desk until he had it right. He had an expensive pen that he took from inside his dark blazer, carefully twisting the cylinder to make the tip appear and filling the page in large and swirly words. It seemed to take a very long time, this story he was writing about you. Once upon a time, you thought. Once upon a time.

You discovered what he was writing only when he paused for a second, and with a distracted look on his face, raised his head and spoke. 'Have you been suspended before?'

'No,' you say, but you'd paused and had to think about it enough that you'd added, 'I don't think so.' He dropped his pen purposefully on his desk and looked you over.

'Well, have you or have you not?'

'No,' you say, but he wanted more and continued to look at you. 'I have not,' you say. He waited a little longer before picking up his pen again and continuing to write. You held his eye, not out of defiance, but because by then your tears had dried and left you exhausted and unable to look away.

When he finished writing, he folded the paper twice with great skill and attention so that the ends came together perfectly.

'I'm suspending you for a week,' he says. He let the words hang in the air while he put the paper inside an envelope. His fat fingers were remarkably nimble.

'However, I'm strongly suggesting expulsion to the Board of Education if you so much as breathe on something that doesn't belong to you here. The guards will also be notified of your criminal activity.' He raised the letter to his mouth, and his wet tongue shot out in small feral licks across the glued edge. Then he pressed the envelope between his thumb and forefinger until he felt the adhesive had bonded. 'I don't want you in my school any longer. I don't mind a chap who is trying and needs help, but you're the worst type of chap, you don't try, Knolls. A thief and a layabout — what use is it having you here?'

You realised it was a real question. You thought to say, 'No use,' so he could make his point and he could repeat, 'No use,' and maybe add, 'At all.'

He took up his pen again and wrote the words '*Mr & Mrs Knolls*' in lovely writing that you'd expect to find on an invitation to a wedding or a funeral. It frightened you. He slid the envelope across his desk using his fingers.

'Give this to your parents,' he says. Even wearing her glasses your mother would never be able to read that writing, and you could already see it passing back and forth between your brothers' hands over the kitchen table.

'And on your way out make sure Miss Jordan has your phone number. I want to speak to your father.'

'We don't have the phone in,' you say and then added, 'We're on the list.' He tightened his mouth and made a sucking sound, drawing air in through his teeth.

'Then give her your address.'

It was a relief to stand and feel blood moving back through your arms and legs. You knew he didn't care so much that he would take the time to come to your house. It almost made you smile to think of your mother scurrying around, trying to match a teacup with a saucer out of the good china, hoping against hope that there was a digestive biscuit left in the house.

'Principal Burke . . . Sir?' you say, after standing a moment in the doorway, feeling the inside of your mouth dry and the words scratching at your throat. He had begun writing again, and he didn't look up, and you wondered if your words had been too weak to find their way across the room to him.

'Do I leave now or after . . . I mean, when do I go, when am I suspended from?' He looked up from his desk, and even from across the room you felt the rage in the slow rise of his heavy eyes.

'Get out of my sight,' he says, sending you past the secretary, the benches, and further out to the corridor, where you were swept along by the burst of students and noise and movement, as if thrown by the final force of a great river before you were deposited out to sea.

22

At Cats' Den you sat with your school bag thrown off to the side. You held the envelope between your fingers and turned it around and around. The paper was heavy and felt nice against your skin.

After lighting your cigarette, you kept the match alive and swiped it quickly past the letter a few times. The corner blackened a little but didn't catch. What if you just didn't show the letter and pretended to go to school every day? You inhaled deeply and were turning the thought over in your head when you heard movement from the bushes below. You saw the white of Sharon's hair bobbing up and down like a buoy in green waters as she made her way up the final part of the steep path.

She saw you, and you could tell that at first she didn't recognise you in the distance and was frightened. She stopped, sharply pulling her head back to focus. Then she turned and spat and sauntered forward with a huff and a puff as if she was murdered by the climb.

She had glasses, Sharon; she had shown you when she first got them, the pink glasses, given for free by the Eastern Health Board. She'd put them on and carefully watched how you looked at her. 'They suit you,' you'd said to her. 'Fuck off,' she says, and you had not seen them since. Sharon, sitting for hours at Cats' Den, near blind with just her smokes and her thoughts for company.

'Fucking wrecked,' she says. 'Giz a smoke or I'll bate you.' She flopped down with her back to the comfy rock and held up her face to the sky. Says, 'Fuck you doing here?'

'You're going to get all wet if you sit there,' you say. She turned and caught you looking to where her black miniskirt had risen up. With both hands she pulled her skirt back down, touched her knees together and sat forward.

'Bit early for you to be here,' she says.

'Yeah.'

'Jaysus, swear your tongue would be reefed out of you if you said anything.' Her tights were shiny, and the light danced up in a straight line along her legs. She'd quickly rolled her cigarette, lit it and left it stuck in her mouth, while her chilled hands were plunged into the pockets of her black bomber jacket. But she couldn't sit that way for long because the smoke kept going into her eye, so she squinted a few times and gave up, taking a hand back out.

'I was suspended,' you say, trying as best you could to make it a careless thing. A thing that didn't touch the inside of you at all.

'What did you do?'

'Stealing,' you say.

'Stealing, stealing what?'

'Bits of bikes.'

'And you were caught? Jaysus, does your da know?'

'No, it just happened.'

'Jaysus . . . ' she says, and you thought how glad you were that she'd come along. This was what it would be like to have someone to confide in; it was a terrible thing to have no one to confide in.

'You big fucking eejit!'

'What?'

'The fuck you get caught for, Sonny?'

'I didn't get caught on purpose.'

'You were only hanging on in there, they can get rid of you now — they can tell the guards and everything.'

'How do you know?'

'Of course I fucking know, what did you think? Everybody fucking knows.' She was really shouting at you.

'You said I should leave. I thought you'd understand.'

'Why would I understand? You're fucking uselesser than me, you get thrown out of there and what? You're fucked, you big thick.'

'Don't fucking call me that!' you say and then your breathing was heavy and that sick fear had returned. Sharon pulled on her smoke a few times through the silence and then threw it away like she hated it.

'I'm off,' she says and went to stand. 'I'm not sitting here with you.' But you didn't want her to stand, you didn't want her to go and leave you alone, so you pushed her before she could get up, and caught her off balance, sending her twisting back to the ground.

'Fucker,' she says, lurching towards you. She threw some punches into your body, and they hurt and were lovely and a comfort. You gathered her closer. And just then, you wanted her. You wanted her to want you too, to satisfy all your longing. You felt empty and sick and aroused.

Her face was moving and blurred and you focused on her mouth and leaned forward, covering her lips with yours. She pushed into you, suddenly. You felt her tongue deep in your mouth, a tooth knocked against another and your mouth was wide open as if you were about to cry out.

You put a hand on her breast and rubbed at it like it was a thing separate from her. There was a tenderness to her face that you couldn't understand. And when you touched her she let you, she just let you. You watched as she unbuttoned your pants and you felt the cold air around your prick. Her fingers drew around you, her chewed nails and the stain of tobacco on her fingers. You kissed her again, breathless, again and again, and the world swelled up in a single noiseless scream, and all that filth and hate and anger spilled from you. Your body falling forward, holding Sharon tightly, immediately you thought of Vera, so deeply that Sharon must have felt it.

She pushed you away from her and sat up; her face was turned from you. Her elbows on her knees, she was pushing the knuckles of her fist into her forehead. It must've hurt. You buttoned your pants with your wet prick showing not a scrap of its former urgency.

You looked over to Sharon and there was mud on the back of her jacket and a stray brown leaf in her hair. You couldn't move towards her.

'You're lovely,' you say, like I'm sorry, but only because you didn't want for her to think what she thought. Her stillness frightened you.

'Do you want a smoke?' you say, and she moved her head enough to acknowledge you without turning. You wanted to see her face and moved around to the other side of her and began to roll her a cigarette while

166

shooting quick looks. You passed her the smoke; she took it in her hand and you lit it.

She drew the smoke deeply inside and looked up at you. 'You got some on me tights, you dirty bollox.'

She reached out and took hold of a clump of grass and reefed it from the ground, then used it to wipe her leg. She took another drag and scattered the grass towards you.

'Here, you have it,' she says and laughed a hollow laugh.

'Was I rough? I'm sorry.'

'Don't care,' she says.

'I'm sorry.'

'I don't care, I said. I don't fucking care.' She looked at you and then off through the brambles.

'What?' you say.

'Does that mean you want to be my boyfriend now?'

You took your cigarette from your mouth and watched it fall to your side.

'Yeah,' you say. She didn't speak then, but a little satisfied smile cut across her face, and she rose her shoulders up once and let them drop with an exhale.

'And I can tell everyone and everything?' she says.

'Yeah, course,' you say.

She looked at you without showing any

hurt and says, 'Suppose you have to say that, don't you?'

'No.'

'Yeah, you do, 'cause I could just tell people you groped me in the bushes and you'd hate that, wouldn't you? Tell them you made me wank you off, forced me. I could call the guards, you'd fucking hate that.'

'Yeah,' you say, feeling the shutters of your eyes heavy; your own cigarette smoke was making you sick.

'When I was suspended. Today. In the principal's office. In front of the prefect. I cried.' It was the most you could admit to her, and later on when you turned it around in sleepless fits, you saw you were telling her she didn't want for a boy like you, not really.

You looked at her for a while, you tried, but you couldn't read her at all. Again you could have told her you were sorry, but it would only have been for you.

'Not surprised, you poof,' she says, and you looked at her two feet before you, and your eyes drifted up along her legs and that place where her miniskirt stopped that had so moved you minutes before, her arse and neck and hands and mouth; you had wanted it all. And after, not even the memory of desire survived.

23

There was the familiar shape of your mother's hunched shoulders, the cold tap pouring over her hands, and the peeling, always peeling. She turned and looked at you.

'Where have you been?' she says. 'I've been waiting to finish up.'

'Joe, he kept me late,' you say.

She turned back to the sink and says, 'I hope he's paying you for that.'

Joe had not kept you late. At the end of your shift, after taking off your apron, you'd gone to wash in the metal sink. There was blood smeared on your hands and up your arm, and more under your fingernails, caked and hardened, and for the first time it disturbed you, it turned your stomach. There was no soap, so you held your arm under the tap and used the old nailbrush. You only felt the pain of the hard scraping brush when Joe found you some time later and says, 'Knock it off, they're bloody clean, all right.'

You pulled a chair out from under the kitchen table, and it stuck into that rip in the lino that had been inching its way across the floor for years.

'Have you homework?' your mother says.

'No.'

'How is it you never have homework?' It was the same conversation you had every night, but it never went any further. You wondered how it must be in other houses, until you looked at your mother at the sink and felt mean for blaming her. She put a plate of chips and eggs on the table in front of you.

'Thanks,' you say and you couldn't begin to understand the sudden emotion you felt for her. Her small gold wedding band was embedded on her ring finger; you'd marvelled at it as a child, how her working hands had swollen, locking the ring, so that it'd been years since she'd removed it. If she wanted to, she never said, and when she died, they'd bury her with it.

She put on the kettle and cleared the potato skins out of the sink. Then she took the red plastic basin from the draining board and flipped it right side up.

'I'll do them,' you say quickly. She paused, holding the washing-up liquid, and looked at you. She had greenish-blue eyes, your mam, and you guessed it was because of the smokes, they had a thin film over them.

'You'll do them?' She knew something was wrong.

'Yeah.'

She laughed through her nose in a breathy way. 'Sure, I'd be quicker doing them myself.' And she rubbed her hands into the tea towel; she was always rubbing her hands like that.

In the morning you could get up and pretend to go to school. Instead you would go to Cats' Den and wait for Sharon and buy her some smokes by way of a sorry. Then you could go and see Joe. You could ask about the apprenticeship, and if he said yes you could tell your mother you'd got the apprenticeship, and then the suspension would matter less, if at all.

It filled you with hope, enough to put a good belt of ketchup on the side of your plate and spread a knife full of butter on the bread for a chip sandwich, and the heat of the chips melted the butter just right and it dripped up your sleeve, so you ate your sandwich with your elbow pointed in the air like an arrow.

'Are you enjoying that now?' your mother says.

'Yes,' you say. It was true because you saw now that everything was going to be all right. There had been no need to cry at the principal's office. And even though you were thinking of Vera when you were with Sharon, it was only because you were in a bad way, and Sharon couldn't have known for sure. You could make up for that in time. Time is a great healer, everyone says so.

You took another slice of bread and used it to wipe your plate clean. You thought about how after Joe paid you, you could pick up something nice for your mother, maybe one of those china figurines she liked. They sold them in Stanley's for two pounds and five pence. You stood and carried the plate to the sink, looking first to her for permission before putting it in. When your hands were free, you threw one arm around her, and hugged her from the side in a joking way. She couldn't hug you back, but she gave a sideways glance and a warm smirk and that was plenty. She could be funny sometimes in a dry way that you liked. She smelled of tobacco and soap; that was how she always smelled, that's how mothers smelled.

24

In the bathroom, with the door locked, you watched yourself in the mirror, playing a game with your face. You made different expressions, to see how tough you could be, what it was like when you smiled; sometimes you would go so far as to kiss your reflection, watching as your face came closer to the mirror with your eyes half shut and everything.

'Sonny!' It was your brother's voice, through the floor from downstairs. It was a serious voice and when it came again, 'Sonny, come down here, now,' you knew something was wrong. In the mirror you could see your scared face.

You unlocked the bathroom door and stood on the upstairs landing, holding your breath to listen, but there was only talk, diluted by the TV, so that by the time it reached you it was just noise. You had taken off your shoes before going into the bathroom, but when you saw them sitting on the step, you reached over and put them on. It was the worst to be in trouble with no shoes on.

Your father gave you a look when you crossed through the living room, a strange look you could not read. At the kitchen table, your mother was sitting flanked by your brothers. She was wearing her glasses and close to her squinting face she held the letter. They felt you come into the room. Your mother dropped the letter onto the table and says, 'What is this?'

You could not speak; her glazed eyes, magnified by her glasses, held you from across the room.

'He's been suspended for stealing,' says a brother. 'That's all there is to it.'

Your mother stood, her fingers rubbing at her thin hair. She steadied herself at the counter, and slammed her hands on the steel draining board: it was loud, bang, bang, bang. She went still then and you could see even your brothers were worried.

'I can't take it, Sonny.' She turned around now with her face flushed and what you hoped to God were not the start of tears.

'Steal? What did you steal?'

Still nothing came from you.

'Sonny answer me.'

'Bikes, bits of bikes,' says a brother, gathering up the piece of paper in his hand but not reading it again because already he had it off.

'What am I going to do with you? It's always this house in trouble, you big thick, could you not leave it well enough alone? Stealing, why stealing?' she says, and when she came over and slapped your face, you did not move.

'What am I going to say to anyone, what do I say when they ask? Everyone will know.' The slap didn't hurt much, but still that hot pins-and-needles feeling was there. She rubbed her hand then as if it was sore, and you wondered if she knew it yet or would later on, before she went to sleep.

'Who would know, Mam? Nobody notices him,' says a brother.

'They know everything in this bloody place. They watch everything. I can't take it now, Sonny, I can't.'

'Get him outta that school and up to work,' says a brother. 'Simple as that.'

'He's lucky it was that school, any other and he'd be getting more than a letter home,' says the other brother. And you instantly saw yourself in the tech, surrounded by bodies and boots and punches. 'Just send a letter, say you're sorry for all the trouble and you've decided to take him out, and that's the end of it. If he doesn't work, he doesn't eat.'

Your mother thought about it a worried moment, and asks, 'Who? Who would write it?'

'I'll write it for you.'

'Would you?' she says.

'Yeah.'

You tried to follow what had been decided for you and then thought you would love to write that letter yourself. Just for the words, one after another in a straight line, all adding up to mean that you had decided.

'Of course if Joe doesn't take him, you're shot, 'cause there's nowhere else for him.'

Your mother looked at the brother; it had not occurred to her. She looked at you then. 'You see the trouble you're causing, the trouble you're bringing to this house. Jesus Christ, Sonny, I could kill you.' Her eyes flicked around the kitchen; she had just remembered some important thing. She rubbed her lips together, turning the thought over. She went to the doorway.

'And of course, I have to take care of everything on my own, because that good-for-nothing just sits there.' Her voice had picked up. She'd found it now. 'Suspended for stealing and you're just going to sit there, that's right, nothing to you,' she shouted into the darkness of the living room. 'It won't be someone else's problem when the guards come knocking.'

And that was it, she had him. You could hear the newspaper crunched and thrown to the floor. There was a flash of fear from your brothers, and your mother had gone silent. At your shoulder, some massive force: it pushed you from your standing position clean into the kitchen where you tripped and landed on the floor. You looked up, and he was standing there, his face red. You scrambled to your feet.

'What did you steal?' says your father, his voice hoarse, and the anger made his country accent jump. 'I said, what? What did you steal?' There was nowhere to go in the small kitchen, and already you could feel the straight of the counter top cutting into your back.

'Do you want me to ask again?' he says.

'Bits of bikes,' you say.

'Show me, where? Where are they?'

You followed him with your eyes as he made his way to the kitchen door and flung it open.

'Come on, now!' he says.

You crossed past him and cowered a little, but he'd never hit you, not that way.

You stood out in the dark shed, unsure. Turning to him, you could only make out the bulk of his silhouette.

'Where?' he says, throwing the heel of his palm into your shoulder. It sent you crashing into the wall. 'Where?'

'There,' you say, pointing to the bike.

'Which part?' he says. You looked over the bike. Which part? The frame you had only stolen a little. You'd seen it locked to a bus stop near Dean's Grange; it had been there for a long time, picked over by thieves, the seats and wheels and guts taken out of it. All that'd remained was the big lock that held the steel skeleton to the bus stop, the chain littered in scars where there had been attempts to break it using a hammer and cold chisel. You had waited until dark one Sunday night. You'd put the frame and lock around your shoulder, found they weren't heavy, and climbed the bus stop. At the top you'd simply pulled the chain over the lollipop head and slid back down with both the bike and lock free. You had carried it home then and slowly, night after night, cut into it with a small hacksaw, counting the back-strokes of the blade. There were thousands before you'd felt the secret satisfaction of having the lock fall away from the frame. Then you had started to scavenge the supermarket car parks for discarded and forgotten parts. The yields had been decent: handlebars, the mudguard, the bike chain all came to you this way. But the good stuff? The good stuff was bought by the parents of your classmates, in fancy bike shops you'd walked into just to see how certain parts fitted together. You were trailed around the shop in an obvious way. Every time you'd gone in it got worse until the fella had just told you not to come back unless you were buying something. It was then that you'd taken to looking at the bikes in the school bike shed. You'd noticed on a ten-speed blue Puma that the saddle was askew. It had bothered you, so you'd straightened it. And upon seeing how loose it was, you'd checked once over your shoulder and in an easy way pulled it free from the bike and put it inside your bag.

'All of it,' you say.

'What?' says your father.

'All of it's stolen.'

'For Jaysus' sake,' he says and looked at you as if he might easily hit you, but instead he lurched forward, the speed of him, picking up the bike and flinging it like a pillow across the shed. It struck with such force into the block wall that it seemed to hover there a moment before dropping in a heap on the floor. The front forks kicked out to the side, and the now misshapen wheel had some spokes spraying out like tiny antennae.

Your father found his lump hammer. It was on the floor beside his spirit level and two blunt steel spikes wrapped in orange string. He picked it up in his good hand and crouched, lifting it high over his head, then bringing it down with all his strength, collapsing the centre tube of the bike frame. It was a satisfying sound, the burst of steel hitting steel like a drum. When he'd finished, he stood, breathless, and looked you over once before throwing the lump hammer to the side and walking past you, past the victory of the silent kitchen. Even from the shed you could hear the weight of his steps up the stairs to bed. He would stay up there for hours, his eyes blinking in the dark, waiting, until it was bedtime for the others, when he'd get up again.

You looked over the bike. You'd never ridden it. It was not yours any more, it was evidence of something.

When you left the shed and walked back into the kitchen, gently pulling the kitchen door shut, no one looked at you or spoke. Your mother carefully kept her back to you.

25

You walked the length of O'Connell Street, up as far as the Gresham Hotel, where you felt protected for the moment by a huge night porter, standing out front like an old centurion on the city walls, in his beautiful long black wool coat and his gloved hands and dark cap. Beyond him you could see the gleam of chandeliers and soft thick rugs. No one you knew had ever stayed there, but there was an aunt — your mother had told you about her — she had had afternoon tea there once and for months after talked about the scent of beautiful perfume and how she'd gone to the toilet without her handbag, and been embarrassed because she had no coppers to leave the attendant.

You stopped a few feet from the porter and used a street light to help you stand. You were drunk on a bottle of Malibu you'd taken from the cupboard in the hall before stealing a final glance at the bike and slipping out unnoticed. You'd walked up the street, aware of how much you had staggered but could do nothing to stop it. You took out your tobacco and with great concentration began to roll a cigarette. A little further up, just off O'Connell Street, the Ambassador Theatre stood like a lighthouse, a final beacon before the blackness of North Dublin.

'Do you want one?' you say to the night porter, holding the misshapen thing in the air first, before putting it to your mouth and lighting it. The porter half smiled, but in a way that let you know he'd only be patient with you for a while. He was about your father's age, but his life had been different, and you could see that by the softness of his face.

'Are you not a smoker?' you say then.

'You've had a few?' he says in an accent the same as your own, only he had broken off a few of the rougher bits.

'Yes, I've . . . had a few.'

When he stood beside you, he kept his body turned so that he was not facing you and could easily watch the glass doors of the hotel.

'Are you not a bit young for that?' he says. 'You're on your way home, I hope?' He was pushing his hands inside the gloves, tightening the calf's leather around his fingers.

'I don't know, I don't think so.'

'Where would you go on a rotten night like this?'

'Just walk around, you know?'

182

'I'd say you'd be an easy target the state you're in.'

'To who?'

'Doesn't matter to who, just that you would.'

'I suppose,' you say. 'I'd be an easy target in any state.'

'You might,' he says. 'Go on and get yourself home.'

'It's the only light on O'Connell Street,' you say, looking across the pale stone.

'Not the only one,' he says.

'The only one like this.'

'You may be right.'

'I have a friend, a woman, she stays here a lot, Vera, Vera Hatton? Do you know her?'

'I might know her face.'

'She's English,' you say.

He laughed at that.

'That doesn't narrow it by much,' he says.

'She's beautiful, she's fucking beautiful.' Your cigarette was spent, so you let it drop to the wet path, and its glow was devoured.

'I'll never stay here,' you say, and when you caught his eye you could see you'd made him uncomfortable.

You launched yourself off the street lamp, back in the direction you'd come from. It was harder to move than before and once or twice your foot slipped from the path and you stepped out onto the road. Further up the street you turned to see his tiny figure, with his arm raised for what you assumed was a taxi.

You stood still and tried to focus. It was the guards pulling up alongside him. The night porter put his head to the lowered window and talked with a hand pointing towards you. It took you a moment, it took the soft lick of a blue light against the walls of the surrounding buildings before you knew to run, turning onto an unknown street until the car slowly passed without seeing your low crouching body in a darkened doorway. You ran on, back over the bridge, where a few stray lights skimmed across the dark top of the river.

★   ★   ★

There were prostitutes along the canal and as you passed them, their faces seemed distorted, gold shining in the flash of car lights.

Further along, the path was deserted, except for one woman who walked towards you like a tightrope walker along the edge of the kerb. When she saw you she moved to a nearby bench.

'Do you mind if I sit?' you say, as you came close to her.

184

'Sit,' she says. She was foreign. She had an accent, but you couldn't find a home for it. 'Do you have money?' she says, looking past you with some curiosity, down the empty street.

'No, no money, but I don't . . . you know,' you say. You sat down on the bench with enough force that the wooden slats sent you bouncing gently for a moment.

She watched a passing car. Two large men sat up front and looked back from behind the glass. The car halted and idled a moment before the driver changed his mind and moved on.

'It's the police,' she says.

'Is it?'

'Look at your face. Yes, it's the police.'

It was quiet then, enough to hear the gentle drift of the canal, its black water heading out to sea.

'I have ten pounds,' you say into the still night, and for a second she seemed as though she had not heard you, and you were not sure you were brave enough to say it again. Then just her eyes flicked towards you, looking at you without looking at you at all.

'Give it to me,' she says. You felt past some coins and bits and pieces to find the old note, and pulled it loose. Without looking at you she took it between her brightly painted fingernails, and it went inside her pocket with her hand.

You looked up the empty street and thought how you'd never seen that street in the daytime and how different it must look with the line of trees and little benches and the canal.

'What do you think for this ten pounds?' She started to unbutton her coat, and she exhaled like a man who has stood up from the table before going out to work, but doesn't want to go to work. Your eyes inched over her, button by button. You could see her bare breast.

'Ten pounds is not so much. You don't get much for ten pounds?' As she reached for you, her scent grew stronger and she put her hand around your neck, squeezed it until it hurt.

Over her shoulder you could see the unmarked Garda car crawling towards you. You saw it, and you didn't care, even though there was still time to pull away from her and save yourself, but you didn't want to be saved, so you reached forward and cupped your hand around her breast, and her skin felt hot and tacky.

When she saw the car she quickly stood and started in a slow jog along the road, disappearing under the shadow of the trees, leaving you alone on the bench.

The car door opened, and two uniformed guards emerged and walked towards you. One of them stopped and raised a foot to the path, leaving the other on the road, a hand resting on his hip as he looked after the fleeing girl.

'She can move all right,' he says in a thick country accent.

The other guard laughed. 'She's like a boomerang, huh? Just give her a few minutes.'

As they came closer to you, you wanted to stand; that's what you'd learned to do. But your limbs felt drained and useless and your head rolled helplessly.

'And what's your story?' says the guard to the right of you, but you didn't answer quick enough for his liking, and his polished boot shone like a jackknife and lashed out. There was a stabbing pain at your shin and you doubled over on the bench.

'I'm sorry, sir,' you say.

'I said, what's your story?'

'I was at a party, sir, and there was wine, and I drank it, and I felt sick and sat down and the lady tried to help, sir.'

'She looked like she was helping all right,' says the other guard, but the tone was different with you then, and you thought it was because you'd called them sir.

187

'On your feet, and away home with you — don't let me see you here again.'

'Yes, sir,' you say, standing. You swayed, stumbled forward towards the guards and fell past them onto your knees and the ground. Above your head you heard one of them saying, 'I have no time for this.'

'Sure, what can you do,' says the other and then, 'Throw him in the back.' You felt their hands at your shoulder, and you were hoisted to your feet.

'If you're sick in this car, I swear to God it'll be the sorriest night of your life.' You were pushed into the back of the police car and felt the engine starting up. The guard in the driver's seat says, 'We're not a bleeden' taxi service . . . It'd nearly be quicker to hold him for the night.'

'We'd have to charge him. Drunk and disorderly, I suppose.'

'Look, sure we'll bring him in and we can decide there,' he says and put the car in gear. It began to creep forward.

'The desk sergeant will still be there.' This meant something to the other. The car was stopped and they looked at each other and one of them adds, 'I could do without that.'

'Where do you live?' he says. When you didn't answer, he turned in his seat, showing you his dark eyes.

'My parents are away,' you say.

'Well, where are you staying? You're staying somewhere.' When you didn't answer the other guard told you that you were trying his patience.

'Monkstown,' you say. 'I'm staying with my aunt on Montpelier Parade.'

26

The roads were damp and empty and the street lights blazed like flares, Ballsbridge, Donnybrook, on out to Blackrock. The coast road through to Monkstown. The Garda car smelled of sweat and something else, maybe piss, but it was not strong. The two guards were silent. A static voice came over the radio occasionally, but they seemed content to ignore it until finally, showing exaggerated effort, one leaned over and turned it down.

The Garda were not to be trusted. Everybody knew that. Pigs, that's what they're called. The prostitute was a pig to them. And you? You had your pigs. You were a pig.

From the Monkstown Road you could see Vera's house on the other side of the old stone wall. You were waiting for it. Waiting to see if a light burned from her bedroom window, two up, one over.

Darkness.

You pushed back further into your seat and let your head fall forward.

'What house is it?' asks the guard, slowing down. How cavalier you'd been, lying to them before.

'This house,' you say. 'Here.' They stopped, headlights illuminating a streak of road.

'She's going to kill me,' you say. 'Can I just go in myself? I won't do it again.'

'We've come all this way, we'll make sure you're left safely inside.'

One guard stood close to your door and waited for the other to walk around before opening it.

'Come on, you,' he says, but you refused to get out of the car.

You sat, a useless lump without a plan, and he reached in and took hold of the hair at the back of your head and pulled you onto the wet path.

'Do ya think I've time to be wasting on you?' you hear him say. 'Now get up to fuck.' You could feel a hand roughly slip under your arm and tuck in at your armpit and you were propelled forward to the granite steps. One held you in place while the other moved purposefully up and located the doorbell. He stood suddenly erect, waiting. You noticed for the first time that he had put his flat Garda cap on and looked very smart.

You watched her bedroom window, watching and waiting for a light to come on, for signs of life. Nothing. The guard reached forward to press the bell a second time, but before he had had time to release his finger, the door swung open, and there she stood. For a moment there was a lovely silence. You searched for her face but found only the outline. She had not been sleeping. She was watching from the darkness.

The guard holding you coughed before speaking.

'Do you know this young man?'

Vera was in no hurry to talk, and you could have curled up and hidden in the space between their words.

'Yes,' she says, simply.

'Well, he says he's your nephew.'

'My nephew,' she says, with what you thought might be the start of a smile, and it gave you hope.

'We picked him up on the canal. Drunk, says he was at a party and drank there, but, the canal, you know, the canal's where we picked him up.'

'The canal,' says Vera.

'He wasn't alone. We're willing to let the matter rest, if we have some assurance from you that he won't be seen around there again.' His arm was still fixed on to you, for support or to stop you running away, you didn't know.

When Vera stepped forward, the light from the main road fell around her. She was lovely, your Vera, even as her open hand lashed across your face.

'He won't be seen around there again,' she says to the guards. You could feel the guard's grip loosen. You walked carefully, steadying yourself, through the door.

'Goodnight,' you heard the guard say behind you and you knew he'd be telling the story later, at the station. 'Oh, a good belt she gave him,' he'd say and laugh all over again.

★ ★ ★

In the hallway you waited, your eyes adjusting to the dark, the way hers must when she moved around at night. You made out the shape of her body, facing you, and her hands tucked behind her back and her shoulders touching the closed door.

'What do you want?' she says, as if there was no answer you could give that would disturb her. It was such a simple question.

'Nothing,' you say with a shrug, then felt disappointment that rose up like the damp. She moved forward and for a moment you thought she'd come to you. But you heard the steel of the latch, and the door was opened, and the night air came and found you.

'I don't know,' you say. 'I don't know what I want.' You moved towards the steps. 'Tell me what.'

193

'Get out,' she says.

You looked outside, the slick empty roads, the tall trees. 'I want to stay, that's what I want. I want to stay,' you tell her. 'Please.'

For the first time you could see her plainly. 'Close the door,' she says. 'And wait in the living room.' She walked past you, up the stairs, and disappeared.

★ ★ ★

Street light came through cracks where the heavy fabric of the curtains didn't meet. You walked around the sofa and lowered yourself into it, listening for the little sounds of her, upstairs. A noise you couldn't identify; perhaps a wardrobe was being opened. Her footsteps were light and deliberate, and you could follow them out of the bedroom, crossing to the other side of the house where you could hear the sound of running water.

She appeared in the doorway holding a small pile of blankets. You stood as she came around the sofa and placed them on the armrest.

'Thank you,' you say. She dropped a pillow at one end, and turned and looked at you.

'You smell,' she says. 'I'd never get the smell of you out of my couch.' She stood at the door, waiting.

194

'Come on.'

You followed her up the stairs, and turned towards the bathroom. You heard the sound of the water stop and the few drips that followed. She was kneeling at the bath when you walked in, her fingers immersed.

The room was not brightly lit, but after the darkness, the two small electric bulbs seemed to glower starkly on either side of the mirror.

'You can hang your coat on the back of the door,' she says, lifting her body off the bath. She turned and stood quite still, watching you.

You removed your jacket, looking away from her, shy, and found the hook. You pretended to make sure the coat was hanging correctly, to give her the time to tell you she was leaving, or not to disturb her sleep when you were done, or one of those things you'd expected her to say. When you turned back around you found her fixed there.

'Undress,' she says.

You looked frightened, you knew that, and your face flushed. You didn't know where to start; you pulled roughly at your belt, unbuckling it, then moved to the top button on your shirt. You saw your hands, your fingernails were nearly black, and you felt all wrong: you couldn't connect them as your own. With the flush of feeling everything was separate.

You undid one button and then the next, and when you chanced a look to Vera and caught her eye by mistake, there was no way of knowing her mind or even guessing at it.

Removing your shirt felt like ripping away the skin of some fruit, and once removed what was left was tender and white and could be crushed with a single thumbnail.

'The floor's fine,' she says.

You dropped the shirt and then dipped down and untied your laces and pulled your boots from your feet. When you unbuttoned your jeans and started to draw down your zip, it came to you; you looked up at her and knew she was punishing you.

You pushed your jeans down your legs to your ankles and in a clumsy way got them over your feet as if you'd never undressed yourself before. When you straightened up, your hands covered your prick, and you stood before her in your underwear. You thought of the night air, that aimless you, walking. Your own bed, the cold sheets and the brothers breathing. You slipped off your underpants and stood naked before her.

She turned slightly to the bathtub and told you to get in, so you crossed past her and one foot, and the next, dipped into the water. It was hot, just under the hot that hurts. You lowered yourself down, feeling the water swirl around your thighs, your hips, the swell of sex.

She took up a bar of soap and a facecloth and kneeled close enough for you to be able to take in every blemish and line and hair. Her left ear had been pierced twice. She rolled up her sleeve and dipped the soap into the water. She wrapped the facecloth around it, told you to lean forward, and when you hugged your knees she started to run the cloth over your shoulders and back; your prick pressing against your stomach.

'Lay back,' she says.

You were not sure, but you thought you heard a softening in her voice. When she reached across you to wash your far shoulder, the fabric of her robe brushed past your face. You watched where her robe fell in a plunge and there was the flash of her white breast. You wanted to reach for her, to pull her close and feel the weight of her body. Her long fingers dipped into the water and she must have felt that.

'Don't,' she says, and you felt the sudden cold of the lit room. She was watching you like some curiosity or specimen, that strange lifeless expression on her face.

At the sink, pulling at a hanging towel, she dried her hands, watching herself in the mirror. Her head bowed forward a little, and she rubbed her eyes as if suddenly tired.

You looked down at your body, the water lapping at your chest, and beyond, your shrinking prick drooped around your pubic hair.

She opened a small green jar she'd taken from the side of the sink and dipped her finger into it. With her eyes to the mirror, she applied it to her face and you could smell it from where you lay, that familiar smell of her, all from a little green jar.

Vera wiped her hands across her face once more and replaced the lid.

'I'm going to bed,' she says with a glance towards you. 'Turn off the light when you're done.'

She looked a moment longer before leaving the room. She pulled the door behind her — it didn't shut all the way — and you could hear her footsteps moving across the landing to her bedroom, where the door firmly closed.

When you stood up the water seemed to crash around you. The mirror had mostly steamed up and reflected fragments of you, here and there. This part and not the other, giving here, but not there.

★   ★   ★

Your jeans stuck to your legs when you pulled them on. You rolled your underpants into a ball and folded them into your shirt, then you tucked them into your big coat pocket. You went back over to the bath and saw that damp film of you, congealed at the bottom, dead skin and hair. Something, however lopsided, was shared, you could see it. You ran the tap, and the warm water washed it away.

At the top of the stairs you held the rail and listened. She knew her own house and must have known you were there. She'd have heard you turning off the light and heard you trying not to be heard coming out onto the landing. You wondered if her eyes were open, listening to what you'd do next, but you guessed she already knew.

You crossed the hallway and felt the cold door handle, turned it and pushed inside. She was lying in the bed with her eyes open, showing no hint of surprise.

'I don't want to sleep on the couch, I want to sleep here, with you.' You didn't wait for a reply; you went to her bed, turned first with some modesty and unbuckled your jeans, sat on the side and slipped them off, listening for her to protest. When she didn't it embold-ened you and you rolled yourself under the blankets and lay facing her. She watched you. Her eyes reflected you back but gave nothing of themselves.

She stretched over and turned out the light, and in the dark bedroom you reached for her. She was naked, and her skin was warm under the blanket. Your hands felt rough on her body. She was unexpectedly slight in your arms and you pulled her to you, and you could feel as she came to meet you.

Her breath changed then, deepened. You could feel the warm air move against your ear, as if you were someone else in her bed. Her hips pushed back at yours. And you were overwhelmed when she told you to kiss her, her voice dry and hungry, and you did and felt her kiss with all that hot breath behind it.

She rose up above you and with your prick in her hand she guided you inside her. She bore down and you felt her all around you. You reached for her face, but she was too far from you. She was somewhere in the darkness, nowhere really.

With a dizzying rush you sat up, throwing your arms around her waist, your face across her breasts, and cried out. She moved her hips a few more times, slowly then, without a hint of that urgency. Her fingers moved through your hair, and already you could feel the weight of her body lifting, leg by leg as she raised herself off you. She sat there, on the side of the bed, with her slow breathing, but otherwise silent and still.

Time passed, probably not that much of it, but it seemed endless to you, wanting to reach over to her, but unable. She turned finally and took up a cigarette and you searched for her face when her inhales sent the tip aglow, and you could still feel sweat thinning at your thighs where she had sat across you, and the room was full of the smell of smoke and sex, and your confusion lingered breathlessly.

She felt your questions mounting and held the last of the cigarette to your mouth and let you take a draw before the spark was extinguished, before you heard her say, 'You should sleep downstairs.'

Her back was turned to you, and you felt her side of the bed sail off into the darkness leaving you adrift.

Out on the Monkstown Road a late-night driver passed, maybe the only sound till first light when the diesel trains would start up, the cars too. You didn't go and sleep downstairs, you reached over and carefully touched her back, moving your fingers over her skin, wanting to remind her in her dreams that you were still there, your hand on her back and the other close to your mouth, so you could smell her sex and know where you had been.

27

You lay awake most of the night watching her, listening to the rise and the fall of her breath, as if sleep was a sharp and dangerous thing. The unhurried seconds, each one slow-birthed and dull, and you waited helplessly for the next. You could see the air changing from black to blue-black and her pale face came slowly into focus.

She had begun to stir in bed as the start of the heavy traffic could be heard out on the road. It wasn't the waking-up type of stirring, but you could wait no longer. You peeled back her blanket and sheet and could feel the warmth of her body escaping. You pressed your head to her breasts, your forehead trailed across her stomach, and your cheek rested a moment across her warm bed of dark hair as you pushed her knees apart.

Sharon Burke had told you about lick-outs. 'Birds love it, drives them fucking mad,' she says. 'But you have to be careful not to try and kiss them right after, 'cause they wouldn't thank you for that at all. Mouth like a bag of gee.'

You could feel the contours of her flesh,

sleek and warm. But even when her sleepy fingers found their way to the back of your head and guided you, and you could hear her breathing into the milk-blue room, you were unsure. You wanted to please her, you were too keen, you were sure you'd blundered it when she pushed you aside, doing with her index finger what you could not and only when she was ready, calling you to lay across her.

Later, she'd got up from the bed and covered herself in her robe and had already tied a first knot in its belt and was about to twist it into a second. You were still on her bed when you say carelessly, 'Will you let me try again?' And you were thinking that you knew her body, naked under that robe, that, although you didn't know it by heart, you knew it a little. She only looked at you and in her own time left the room, taking the air with her.

You heard her pissing and then the bathroom tap running. The thought of morning-cold water sent a chill through you. There was an unexpected burden you carried now in a sharp casing somewhere under your ribs and at the top of your stomach. Emptied of sex and wanting, what remained of you felt like it could be knocked to dust if Vera so much as smiled at you. You sat on the bed and waited for the sound of the bathroom door opening and her footsteps across the landing before she went downstairs.

★ ★ ★

'I'm not well,' says Vera, but you knew that, even you who knew so little. You were sitting at the kitchen table with the smell of fresh coffee in the air, trying to seem as if what had happened had not changed you in some way, however small or large. She put a mug in front of you, and you wrapped your hands around it without any desire to drink. You looked up at her, could only hold her eye for a moment before looking away. You felt the heat through the ceramic mug burn at your palms.

'About the guards and all, sorry for that,' you say. She sat across from you, staring, her full mouth close to the rim of her cup.

'Is there anything else you want to apologise for?' And you thought about breaking into her house and Sharon and all the things Vera didn't know about. You thought about rummaging at her sex that morning and what a terrible thing for her to feel, when you'd forgotten yourself and thought she had felt as you did.

'I'll make a list,' you say. And you thought

she smirked a little; you could see a criss-cross of lines at her eyes.

'Don't apologise,' she says.

'Are you afraid?' you say.

'Afraid? Why would I be afraid?'

You couldn't say why, but just stared at her until she understood.

'Oh, I see. You're trying to be delicate.' She looked off as if remembering something. 'We're bookends, you and me, do you know what I mean? When you think, you think forward, you think about the future. I think backwards, I think . . . ' She rested her cup on the table and wouldn't tell you what she thought.

'Thanks for the coffee,' you say after a while.

'Of course, you're welcome . . . No, no, I'm not afraid.'

You wanted to say that that was good, or that you were glad, or something, but you were so unsure.

'What are you thinking?' you say finally. You'd seen it on the television a few nights ago. Some American show where they kept asking each other what they were thinking. She ran her hands over her face and forehead as though forcing herself awake.

'Mind your own business,' she says and she smiled. Everything about her was sad, but mostly when she smiled.

'Why don't you have a husband?'

'Chatty fucker in the morning, aren't you?'

'What did you expect, riding a youngster?'

'Oh God, I think I'm going to be sick.' She sat back in her chair, taking a cigarette from her packet and letting it hang between her fingers, then reached for some bread and roughly pulled away the crusts and put some cheese on it.

'How old are you?' she says, but it didn't interest her much. 'No,' she says then.

'No?'

'No, you don't get to ask me anything.'

'Why not?'

'Because that's not what this is.'

'What is it?'

'I don't know. A very poor idea, probably.'

'I'm telling you nothing, so.'

'You don't have to, I already know.'

'I might surprise you.'

'Go on then, surprise me, shock the shit out of me.' She laughed, as if her body was remembering some old laughter, and you knew she had gone to a school like yours and smelled nice and been beautiful and was liked.

'You're right, I don't think I can surprise you,' you say.

'You're decent, and that's always a surprise

. . . I've had two, if you must know.'

'Two husbands?'

'Yes, two. The first time I was married, I was young, not so much older than you. It was beautiful at first, then sad. But mostly quick. The second time was beautiful too, then sad, and it took a long time.' You knew it wasn't the first time she had said it.

She rested her elbows on the table and dropped her head forward, rubbing the back of her neck with her flat hand.

'Can it ever be beautiful without being sad?' you say.

'God, I hope so . . . for some people I'm sure but . . . Not for me, clearly,' she says.

There was silence then, and it was the lovely kind. Smoke drifted from the tip of her cigarette, forgotten, until she killed it against the glass of the big ashtray.

'Why did you ask me to do the work? If you knew . . . '

'I think you may be in over your head, here.'

'But why?' You thought that she wasn't going to answer, that she was telling you she was done.

'I think one should be expected to leave things at least how they found them, if not better. It's old-fashioned, I know, but I love this house.'

'But you didn't wait.'

'No.' She blinked, then shut her eyes and there was a tear. It fell against her face before it landed on the table.

'I'm sorry,' you say quickly. 'You don't have to tell me.'

'It's not that . . . it's . . . I'm not well,' she says. 'I have this illness, motor neurones. Do you know what that is?'

'No,' you say.

'It's . . . There's no cure, it sort of kills you from the inside out,' she says sharply, in what sounded like the beginning of a laugh. 'Your heart is the last to go, so you live through the shutting down of your organs . . . I mean, for Christ's sake.' She looked around her, finding her bearings. 'You're paralysed, waiting, fully conscious. Can you imagine? And they say there's a God.' She looked down at the table and her tears were free-falling now. She wiped at them with the back of her hand and dried her hand off her robe.

Both of you looked to vague areas of the room where the other was not. You could hear nothing of the road from the cocooned kitchen, and the garden was still. In the summer, the shutters would open and there would be plants and shrubs and an occasional finch or robin making some noise.

'You can ask me anything,' you say.

When she spoke, her spit thickened the corners of her mouth.

'Light me a cigarette,' she says.

You went to the counter and found them, then sat back down in the chair next to hers, pulling hard on the smoke. She took it from you but never drew on it. Her head rose up from the cradle of her hand and drifted back, searching for somewhere to rest on your body, and you felt the weight of her skull settle into your neck. She twisted the cigarette between her fingers and stared into the room.

'You have to promise not to interfere. You need to promise that.' You could feel the warmth of her body pass through the fabric of her robe. You pulled her towards you, and as if she was chuckling her body shook.

'You should eat,' you say after a while. 'Toast, with real butter, I'll make it.'

'No. No, thanks.'

The coffee had cooled, and it tasted bitter to you.

'I'll make you toast,' she says. 'I'd like to.' She stood slowly. You watched her move with her back to you; she seemed solid on her bare feet. You thought of her insides, each worried organ fretting under the strain of her making toast.

You were in love with her. The realisation

came to you for the first time in words, that that was the feeling you had; you saw you'd fallen in love. It was a shock.

28

Vera insisted on driving you home. You had protested, but she wouldn't hear of it, and your heart fell at her seeing what a small place a small person like you could be from. She kept her car parked in the lane behind her house, where there was a row of wooden A-framed sheds; each house had its own. She opened the little padlock after trying several keys and joked about how often she drove. Then she pulled out in an old cream Renault, which suited her. She shrugged, catching your eye, and smiled lightly.

She wore a pale yellow scarf around her neck with a fleck of green the same shade as her eyes, and she stopped where you were waiting in the lane. She looked like a film star. On the passenger side, empty cigarette packets and paper dockets and receipts spilled out of the door and glove compartment. There was a forgotten lipstick that would roll with the car's motion around your feet. You pulled the door closed behind you and Vera turned and cocked her head towards her shoulder, watching you, and you didn't look away then, you couldn't.

'Where to?' she says.

'Left on the Monkstown Road,' you say.

She held your gaze in what you thought might have been amusement before looking back to the road.

Her bare knees were exposed between her raincoat and winter boots, and you wanted her again, but she was on the other side of giving or taking now. She was stalled, like a sailboat on a windless day, and had no way to move forward.

Vera's car pulled into the housing estate and her face did not change though the landscape did. You watched her as the cars began to thin, the grass along the side of the road rutted in places and overgrown in others. Already, as the Renault idled, a group of teenagers up at the green were watching, and one started to move towards the car.

'Drive straight, don't stop,' you say, without looking at her, your hand moving to open the door.

'I'll be all right, Sonny,' she says. Then she took your arm before you could leave, squeezed it, drew you back towards her.

'I'll be all right, don't worry,' she says, and she smiled at you, but you both knew there was not a scrap of truth to it. Then she reached up and touched your face and says, 'Thank you.'

You thought of her driving home alone, the wipers pushing the coming rain like the unsure hands of a clock, and her putting the little car back behind the wet padlock, her running out of the rain to the big empty house where she'd find her plate and two used cups still on the table, the ashtray full, the unmade bed.

When she had gone, you walked to your front door. Your mother had already unlocked it and it swung a few inches open. When you went in you thought you'd find her, ready in the hall, but Vera's car had thrown her, and she'd withdrawn into the kitchen to rehearse. It was tiny, your house. It must always have been, but you saw it clearly then.

'Where have you been, Sonny?' Her voice was room-level, and you saw she wanted you to hear the strain of it, but it was too late, she'd had too long to think about what she would say. It was not all her fault, she was only half upset and only talking to a half-person, for at least as much of you had stayed behind.

'I stayed with a friend.'

'A friend? What friend?'

'You don't know them,' you say. Your mother had always been the easiest person you knew to lie to; she was willing to be convinced.

213

'Your father was furious this morning looking for you — he wanted you working with him this week.' She looked away then, because you both knew she was lying too. 'Why was that woman driving you?'

You walked around her and picked up the kettle, holding it under the cold tap.

'I asked you a question,' she says. For a moment you thought about telling her; you were full of things you wanted to tell. There was nobody. Nobody.

'She's the woman I was doing some work for.'

'I know who she is — what does she want with you?'

You began to open the presses as if looking for something.

'We've become friendly,' you say.

'Friendly?' she says after you, as if learning the word, and for the first time her mouth curled around it. 'What in God's name does a woman her age want to be friendly with a young fella for? There is something off there, Sonny, I'm telling you now.'

'There's nothing off. She's not from here, that's all, she doesn't know anyone, is all.'

'Careful, Sonny.'

'Ah, stop, would you? Careful? Careful of what?' You sat down then. When you heard the kettle click off you didn't go to it.

214

'They pretend to let you in with them, but you can't be let in with them. You'll get ideas, Sonny, ideas that hurt you. Don't scoff at me, I know what I'm talking about now.' Her voice softened.

'No one's giving me ideas,' you say, but you couldn't look at her.

'Listen to me now, listen. I'm only saying it because I don't want to see you get hurt. I see you there, I see you, sitting there and dreaming of all the things in the world you can never have. That woman will make a fool of you, Sonny, giving you ideas. You wouldn't thank me later if I said nothing and I can't stand to see my children made a fool of, Sonny, I can't.'

Your mother. Not so many years ago you would race home to her after school, just to know she was still alive and hadn't left you in that house of men, without a soft thing in the world.

The kitchen felt like it had never been warmed.

'No one's making a fool of me,' you say, but already a small pool of doubt had crept under your words.

'I don't know what's going on, and I don't want to either.' She held her right hand in the air to stop anything you might say. 'But I know this, a woman her age has no proper business around a young fella. She just doesn't now, do you hear me?'

You'd seen only one early photograph of your mother, covered in dust on top of the wardrobe in her room, her and your father on their wedding day. They were both smiling, but you could see it was because the man taking the picture had told them to smile. You thought if they were just let be they would probably have smiled anyway, but now they had been told, their smiles were empty and shy.

'I've been thinking, Sonny, the best thing you can do is go and see Joe. He's a good one to train with and he's fond of you. Look, when your brothers worked there he always said there was an apprenticeship if they wanted it and I'm sure he'd do the same for you. He would, Sonny, I know it.'

'I don't want to.'

'Look it, what else? What else are you doing? Forget school, you're wasting your time, just wasting it. It's time to grow up now, Sonny.'

You left the house not long after telling your mother you would speak to Joe, and it seemed to settle something, enough that she lit a cigarette, but when she asked you not to be around That Woman, you fell silent again. She let it rest in her way; her mouth tightened, and her eyes were low in their disappointment.

'An apprenticeship, that's it, sure — you can go anywhere with an apprenticeship.'

29

You worked with your father that week. There was a garden wall to build, six foot high with cinder blocks. The family were so upset with their neighbours that they were shutting off their own view of the Dublin Mountains because it included them. Your father doled out the story in dribs and drabs, but you never learned the exact cause of the offence. Several hundred blocks had been dropped off at the kerb and needed to be brought around to the back garden by wheelbarrow. You could only load five at a time; you'd tried more, but the wheelbarrow kept tipping over after a few steps, the blocks crashing to the ground, chipping and breaking. As you walked back and forth, counting each step one to forty, the single wheel drawing the same line with muck, you slipped and exhaustion took hold of you and you found a dull pleasure in that.

It had rained all week, and the job became increasingly difficult. When the rain made the cement too soupy to be workable, your father would stand under the eaves of a garden shed, and light a smoke and stand showing his teeth to the sky. He'd shout at you then to get in outta the rain, and you went and stood beside him, with great drops at your feet, your clothes damp, and tried to shake the shivers from your body.

The few things that weeks earlier you would have talked about with your father, you now found yourself with no heart to ask at all, and so you stood, sometimes for hours, waiting for the weather to pass.

When the last row of blocks was laid, it was raw and ugly, the natural grey made darker by the rain. During the afternoon, you had caught your father looking at you sideways, then down in confusion, and when his head came up again you were sure he was worried. And, for a moment, it felt like he might ask if you were all right or something, but then he was distracted by the cement hardening in the mixer and told you to start cleaning it before it was destroyed.

★　★　★

Your suspension ended and you walked back to school, as unsure as on your first day. You sat through the morning class, watchful, tense, dreading the eleven bell, when you were given a twenty-minute break to walk around with a purpose, even though you had none and were just pretending and listening for the bell that would gather everybody back inside. There was the crack of the classroom speaker, and the thin voice inside called your name, not to the principal's office but immediately to see the school counsellor, Jane. The classroom fell silent. Rumpled bodies twisted to see you.

The door to Jane's office was open, and you could see the lamplight drifting out, different from the strip-lit corridors. You stood at the doorway, looking in at the tiny windowless room. Jane was bent over some papers on her upholstered chair. She had no desk, nowhere to put one, and you thought she seemed exposed. You wondered if she went home at night and told someone she'd love a desk, that she prayed for one, and while she was praying, a window too.

If she felt you standing there, she didn't look up. You knocked at the side of the door, and she glanced at you then, indicating where to sit before going back to her paper, finishing up a word or two and carefully replacing the lid on the pen and putting it alongside the two other pens on her side table. Then she closed the red folder she had been writing in, and you saw your name written in careful letters at the top left-hand corner.

'You were suspended?' she says.

'Yes.'

'For stealing?'

'Yes.'

'You stole from another student?'

'Yes.'

'I don't know what else you expect this school could do for you. You're invited in, made welcome and now as it turns out you are a thief.' She held there and waited until you looked away. 'What happens now?' she says.

Your eyes fixed on the brown carpet tiles, where one tile on the floor had been replaced and was a few shades less faded than the others.

'Oh, for God's sake, Sonny. You're simply wasting — '

But she didn't get any further; you cut her off and shocked yourself when you said, 'I want to be a painter.'

'A painter?' she says. And then she looked at you anew and says, 'Oh.'

It seemed, after saying it, to make some sense. You were good with your hands, you knew that, and once had been even complimented by Mr Williams, the art teacher, and that made you hopeful. You thought back to walking through the hushed halls of the National Gallery and imagined how a place like that could feel like home.

'Well,' says Jane. 'I can see that.' And for

the first time ever she looked at you with some understanding, and it meant the world to you. You would tell Vera. She knew all about painting; she could tell you how to get a start and maybe write you a letter. She would, of course she would. One of those letters that say, 'Sonny Knolls is personally known to me.' You felt something lift inside for a moment; you felt that things might go all right for you after all. You even felt that in that lightness things might go all right for Vera too, that maybe she wouldn't have to die, that now you would have the strength to help her, even where the doctors couldn't. You could bring her to Knock or Lourdes.

'Let's think then, how to make this work for you,' Jane says.

And you trusted her enough to tell her, 'I have a friend, she worked with painters and that, she'd help, I think.'

'Well, you shouldn't have to go too far, your father's in the building trade, he must know painters.'

'My father?'

'I think the best thing to do is to notify the principal that you will be leaving school to find an apprenticeship. Do it before your exams and I'll see if I can secure a recommendation. It won't be easy.' She was reaching again for the folder and a pen.

'I don't want to paint walls,' you say. Your throat was suddenly coarse; you tried to swallow, but nothing came. She held the folder on her lap, half opened.

'What did you want to paint?'

'Pictures.'

'Pictures?'

'Yes, paintings, you know?'

A full breath pushed out of her body in a stifled laugh, and her mouth remained open like fish on the harbour wall.

'Do you mean an artist?' But because she'd used that word, you couldn't say yes. You saw it then the way she saw it.

'Well, that's just ridiculous,' she says, opening the folder fully. 'However, I do think we should . . . ' She began writing and paused until she had finished. 'Pursue a painter's apprenticeship.'

'I don't want to paint walls.'

When she looked up at you this time she was nervous. 'Don't you dare raise your voice in here.'

You hadn't known you'd been shouting the first time, but the second time you did. 'I don't want to paint fucking walls.'

'Don't you — ' But she never finished. You stood up and walked quickly out of her office. Later, when your knuckles bled and your face bled and you were glad of so little, you would at least appreciate that you had stood up slowly from the chair and left Jane's room untouched.

You would hardly remember the walk through the corridors, A and B and C, the throng of students with their screeches and shouts. You pushed your way out past the double doors, filled your lungs with crisp cool air, and it was a relief. The budding trees and ivy. The blueness of the sky and the thought that it was done. You'd never come here again.

You could see the school gates from where you stood and made a first step towards them, turning in an almost sentimental way to look for the last time around the yard. That's when you saw him, the prefect, Graeme. He was marching purposefully, and when you searched around there was only you he was marching towards. You knew the look of boys when they wanted to fight. He had friends trailing quickly after him, mouths open with delight. He stepped in front of you, pushing the palm of his hand into your shoulder, and sent you stumbling backwards, where you found that more students had gathered. You could feel their hands on your back before you were thrown again towards Graeme.

'Ya thieving knacker,' he says, his face close

enough for you to catch the last heat from his breath. You could see, plainly, that he hated you. You had assumed that all his previous hostility towards you had been a game to him, and in part a show for his friends, but this boy, this stranger really, he hated you. And it made you freeze with confusion, so that Graeme could cock his head backwards and say, 'He's going to cry now.' You could hear laughter around you. Students craning their heads around one another so they could be the ones later to say for sure what had happened. It was then you clearly saw Graeme pull his right arm back. He was about to punch your face. You thought he would only hit you once, you knew you could take that, it would satisfy him and his friends of victory, and then you could go. You knew that there would be no fight. You were so afraid of his hatred that you had already lost. Given up.

The punch must have landed just where Graeme wanted it to; it was a great punch, falling just between your cheek and jawbone. You felt your neck pull to the right as your head jerked abruptly, then you waited for the pain that should follow it. You could taste the blood in your mouth and wanted to spit, but you felt no pain.

The crowd was still then; it was a real fight,

with real punches, and they were lost to the sport of it. You stood, blinking dumbly at Graeme, having absorbed the blow. But his same right hand pulled back again, and you saw how it was with him. He needed a bloody win, one that would end with you skidding like a loose stone across the tarmac.

The second punch didn't land nearly so well as the first and his fist rolled off your chin towards your shoulder. So he reached with his left and grabbed on to a tuft of your hair and pulled you towards him and began firing his fist over and over into your face. He was bigger than you, Graeme; his frame was thick. In the breathless grapple, your face touched his, his skin on your own, and for a moment it felt almost tender. He'd grown tired and still the pain you'd expected didn't come. His boxing became more wayward; he was grunting at each punch, but they were growing softer. It was then you thought to push him off you and just make a run for it; you pushed him with surprising ease.

You had never hurt anyone that way. It made you sick to see boys beaten on the ground, that way you'd seen other boys hit with joy. So you were shocked to see your own clenched fist banging at his face.

The years working for your father had paid dividends, the thousands of grey blocks,

Portland cement by the ton, the shovel, the pick. You saw your body was tight and strong and agile; this boy you were fighting saw it, he showed you in the fear in his eyes, and you took it as an invitation to hurt him.

You smashed his face and felt nothing for the pain he felt, even when he dropped to the ground and you raised your heavy boot over his body and stamped on it like it was nothing at all, as if you yourself had never felt pain in your whole life.

Blood came in a steady stream from the prefect's nose, diluted at his chin by tears, and you looked up for the first time at the growing circle of clean faces, dozens of eyes peering down, looking from your raw fists to his badly beaten face. There was no laughter in them, and when you stepped back from Graeme's body, his friends knelt at his side. You turned away, and a path quickly opened for you as the students stepped silently away, and you moved through the corridor of bodies three or four deep towards the school gates.

30

A few hundred yards from the school grounds, the first pulsing pains set in, mostly under your left eye, then around your cheekbones and jaw too. Your knuckles ached, though the blood that smeared across them was not just your own.

Your school bag was missing, flung aside during the fight: some textbooks, English, maths maybe, and geography? The school paid for them through a government scheme. At the beginning of the year, your name and the names of a dozen others had come over the intercom — to come to the library to pick up your books — and the pairs of worn shoes had stood single file, each student knowing the other but careful to look away until the parcels were handed over. Then you could return to class with the books hiding inside your bag.

* * *

Vera slowly opened the door and, seeing your face, she says in a distracted way, 'You're bleeding.'

At the kitchen sink she washed you with warm water and a soft cloth. Her face close to you, close enough that you imagined her breath on your exposed neck.

You checked more than once in the mirror and decided the bruising suited you. It transformed you and for a moment you could see a new person. But even then, as you watched, you descended into something familiar.

It would be the second time you'd spend the night. You weren't sure she wanted it, but when it had got dark and late and you made no move to leave, she never objected. So you sat on the blue couch with her across from you, a book in her hand and a blanket pulled up over her legs. She had lit a fire around six, and there was a timid glow that would rise and fall, but it never really took. You assumed the wood was damp, and this probably was the first fire set in a long time. She had lit it for you, and that warmed you. From two speakers set on opposite sides of the room came a crackly recording of old-fashioned music, with trumpets that had never heard a story end well, and a steady slow drumbeat, but no words. She had asked you if you liked it, and you didn't think she believed you when you'd said yes. But you did like it. She asked if you were not bored. You'd chosen a book too, a book to impress her, but you were too distracted and it sat open on your lap.

The world outside was lost to you, and even the occasional noise on the street was a distant thing. You knew your name was being called in your house, and you knew of the terrible words that would follow your name. You would have to pay for all this, probably soon, but there was time to be frightened of all that.

It had been dark for hours when the book she had been holding dropped on her lap and she watched you for a while.

'Don't have long, you know that?' she says.

'Long?'

'You know what I mean.'

'There's been miracles at Knock, people have been cured.'

'Do you believe in God?' she says.

'I don't know, too scared not to.'

'I don't have the faith for a pilgrimage.' She was smiling. 'But you're welcome to pray for me . . . if the spirit moves you.'

She dropped a narrow bookmark on her page and carefully put it to the side.

'I'm going to have a bath,' she says. Before leaving the room, she knelt down close to you and softly kissed you on your mouth. You touched her face and kissed her back like you'd been doing it all your life.

'It's nice you're here,' she says with mild surprise. She paused then and you knew there was something else she was thinking. You had wanted to say that it was nice to be here too, but because she had said it first it seemed false, and polite for polite's sake.

You couldn't wait long in the sitting room before going upstairs, just long enough to hear the running of the water stop and imagine she had settled herself into the bath. There was the smell of some flower, maybe lavender or rose or some less common one you didn't know. Here and there, a shimmer of light when she moved even a little. She was like one of those ghostly paintings you'd seen in the gallery, laid out, delicate in the bath, as if all her strength was gone.

Her loose wrist hung over the side and there were scars, up and down; scars that criss-crossed like the intersections of roads on a map. You thought of young Milos in the book you'd borrowed, who'd opened his veins in the warm water of a bath.

'What happened?' you say.

'I fell on a banana skin.' She'd said this before and didn't need to open her eyes to know what you were asking.

'What happened?' you say again.

'I fell off my bicycle.'

231

'Vera?'

'I was an angry teenager, and that's all you're getting.'

31

There was nothing left for your mother to say when you showed up, so early in the morning it was still dark outside and would stay dark for some time. She couldn't feign shock, even at you coming through the kitchen window. You had exhausted her, and it galled you to know this and know too that you could've helped her but that you would not.

'Where have you been?' she says. Then she saw your bruises and says, 'Jesus, Mary and . . . What? What happened?'

'I'm all right,' you say.

'You're not all right.' She looked away from you and sat back down with her fingers running nervously across her cigarette packet, sipped her tea and smoked.

'I'm sorry,' you tell her.

'Sorry,' she says. 'Sorry's your middle bloody name.'

You made a cup of tea and sat with her, but there was never time, and it wasn't long before you heard the bodies upstairs moving, sleepy feet pushed inside boots, heavy footsteps to the bathroom. The small and silent space you shared with your mother, before the first brother appeared in the kitchen, was still a comfort. Even when, out of the blue, she says, 'It's that woman. Isn't it?' But you wouldn't give Vera up. You believed in her and nearly told your mother so.

You went upstairs to keep out of the way, until the time you would normally leave. Then you pretended to go to school, but you were going back to Vera.

She had left the latch unlocked. You pushed the back door open and found her curled up in her bed, her limbs heavy with sleep. You undressed and slipped in beside her. You ran your hands across her body, feeling for the pendulum of her breasts, and she reached for you, pushed her warm backside towards you, until the shapes of your bodies were the same, and when you entered her she moaned as if from her dreams.

Vera slept, and light licked the wall across the room. You could hear someone walking past outside.

'Vera, I think I love you,' you say, but you knew she was asleep.

You felt your eyes heavy and you gave in to tiredness, asleep with your fingers inside her, and when you woke it was evening and you'd missed the butcher shop. Your knuckles were pressed against her thigh. Sleepily she moved her hips.

'I think years from now you'll understand this and hate me for it,' she says, still moving. She closed her eyes and pushed her head into her pillow.

'I hate you now,' you say.

'You worship me,' she says, turning to check your expression.

'Worship? Go on and shite,' you say.

'You worship all right, you're blinded by it,' she says. Her eyes, even when she smiled, always stayed some other place, somewhere serious. She touched your face. 'You watched me sleep this afternoon, I felt it,' she says. She got out of bed and stood at the window, pulling the curtain aside; the street light rushed around her. You could see the perfect shape of her thighs, inches apart, her mound of hair through her transparent slip. You knelt behind her and pushed her slip around the curve of her body. You could feel your knees pressed into the uneven floorboards.

★   ★   ★

There was no fire lit that evening. You'd made toast and found a can of beans. When Vera refused hers, you let it go cold and then ate it anyway. A first bottle of wine had been opened at five and then a second and a third. There was a book on her lap, but it lay fallow.

You made attempts at talk but her eyes rolled towards you like warning shots.

In the kitchen, opening the wine, you saw that the bottles of tablets had multiplied. They weren't exactly hidden, but discreetly tucked out of the way. You'd been told not to interfere, but you did.

After Vera's eyes closed you carried her upstairs to bed. You came back to the kitchen and pulled apart the capsules, roughly half of her medication, throwing their powder into the bin as your hand shook, and replacing it with plain flour.

The same doctor's name appeared on every bottle, along with an address.

32

The doctor's office was off Mount Merrion Avenue, in a building not unlike Vera's. It had a separate entrance with a polished brass nameplate outside. You went down some steps to what would once have been called the cellar and were buzzed through into a small empty waiting room. There was no one to ask if you had an appointment, so you sat and waited and tried to decipher the muffled voice of the doctor in the next room.

After a short while the door opened and a man came out, thanking the doctor and pressing a white tissue to his left ear, holding his head at a peculiar angle as he made his way towards the exit. The doctor emerged, very tall in a dark blue suit, the softness leaving his face as he looked towards you.

'Can I help you?' he says, and you found yourself standing quickly; it felt deliberately rude not to, and you didn't want to be rude.

'Yes,' you say.

'Do you have an appointment?'

He was already making his way to the door, to open it for you to depart. You had tried to rehearse it on the way there, to find a way to have some authority over the doctor. You knew he'd ask if you had an appointment, but beyond answering no, you'd found nothing.

'You'll need to make an appointment,' he says.

'I'm not sick. I'm here about Vera Hatton.' He stopped then, stood and looked at you all over again, and you saw how Vera aroused a curiosity in others.

'Who are you?' he says.

'She's lots of tablets from you.'

'What? Who are you, I said?'

'I don't want you giving her any more.' His hand was gripping your shoulder, hard. He had perfect doctor hands and nails, with a small ink stain near the top of his index finger.

'The nerve of you! Who the hell do you think — ? Does Vera know you are here?'

He was handsome, the doctor, older than Vera. Very well preserved — it's good breeding, that's what your mother would have said. You were suddenly jealous of him, the easy way he used her Christian name. He probably had books too, and they could laugh about things from afar and know the things they knew. Vera couldn't talk to you the way she could talk to him. She had to dim herself down so you could see. She had to point and grunt the way you give a foreigner directions

238

and her silence was proof she was becoming bored.

'I'll burn your fucking house down,' you say, quiet enough for him to believe you.

'I'm calling the guards,' he says, letting go of you and walking backwards towards his office.

33

'You're not bleeden' here. I mean, you're here, but you're not here, ya know?' says Mick, sharpening his knife on a steel, four or five quick, even strokes. The sound cut through you. He bent over the butcher block and began to sever the white fat and heavy sinew from around a lamb's neck.

'I mean, I don't give a shite what's going on with you, not really. You show up some days, you don't show others. You know what I mean? Young lads come in here every day looking for a job, I'll tell you something, they'd show up to work if they were given a chance.' He was a good butcher, Mick. His knife glided cleanly, fast cuts, nothing of the meat wasted.

'Anyway, any more fucking about and you're out on your ear, do you hear me?'

'Yeah.'

'Do you?'

'I do, yeah.'

'There'd be no apprenticeship then. Go on, now.' He pointed his knife towards your work.

You went out into the shop, holding some scrunched-up pages of newspaper and the bottle of blue window cleaner. There were no customers. Joe stood behind the counter, staring. When he saw you, he blinked a few times, and started rearranging the display case. He didn't talk to you, and would wait in the back when you were leaving. He was distancing himself from you, so that by the time he was letting you go it would be easier for him.

It only took a few passes to clean the glass counters. Smudges and fingerprints were scarce. You went outside to sweep up the path. It had been dark for a while, and when you turned and looked back inside, Joe and Mick stood shoulder to shoulder, arms folded. The wet ground made the sawdust stick, and you spent longer outside, moving the brush towards the road.

When you looked across the rush-hour traffic, there, standing straight, with her hands deep inside her rain mac, was Vera. You didn't wave or nod or even remember to be embarrassed of your apron and brush. You stared past the moving head-lamps, searching for signs, but she stood and shyly took one hand from her pocket and waved. It filled you with something that wasn't happiness but better. She pointed to the ground she stood on; she'd wait there until you were done and all your worry about the doctor calling disappeared.

When you went back inside, the shop had changed. The weight of Joe's disappointment no longer mattered. You whipped through your work, knowing that they saw the change in you too.

'That's the glass and outside finished, Joe,' you say. 'Is there anything else?'

'No, nothing.' His eyes were wide at the boldness of you.

'All right so,' you say and went into the back room and swapped out your apron for your coat. Mick followed you then and asks, 'Where you off to?'

'Home,' you say, not looking.

'I've been married fifteen years, and I've never gone home that excited.'

'You must be going to the wrong house,' you say.

'I know what you're up to,' he says, and you spun around to him. 'Hanging around with that posh bird, everyone knows, sure the bleeden' dogs are barking it on the street. You'd want to watch yourself,' he says.

'Watch myself?'

'Come on. What would a bird like that want with you? She's using you, I don't know what for but she's using you for something. Watch yourself now, I've seen it happen, a fella throws it all away for a bird and he's left with nothing. I'm only saying, I've seen it happen.'

'Don't have anything to throw away.'

Vera was still there like a butterfly pinned by its wings. You crossed the road quickly and went to her. She kissed your mouth, and her lips were cold; she slipped her arm under yours and you began to walk.

'I realised I hadn't left the house for so long, so I went for a walk and here I am,' she says, her voice bright, and you saw that was how it was for people, not just waiting, but waiting for each other.

'How was work, dear?' she says in a mock old-fashioned way, and you'd watched enough black-and-whites with your dad to know just the answer.

'Swell, dear, just swell,' you say.

'I baked a pie today, dear, I do hope you like it.'

'Well, that's just dandy, dear. Why, I'm sure I will.'

Her heels clicked on the wet path and now and then there was a faint drift of her perfume, or just the smell of her soap, you weren't sure, but it came to you in these little waves. And the longer she held your arm the more you could feel the heat from her body and maybe she could feel the heat from yours.

You turned the corner and plain as day you recognised the shape of your mother, struggling out the door of the Spar shop, with four or more plastic bags pulling at her left and right like demanding toddlers. She seemed to stumble when she looked up and saw you, as her eyes flicked between you and Vera. If Vera noticed, she never said, but you were sure for a moment you felt her body tighten at your side.

You never broke stride. Your mother saw you weren't stopping and jerked her head in an ugly movement towards the ground. You walked on. The cars were fewer then, and across the road, floodlights were thrown over the church's empty car park. A few dim night lights could be seen inside. It was only then you allowed yourself to look back, in time to catch what was no more than a shadow of your mother's narrow shoulders, her slow, small steps.

Vera's house was cold when you got inside. Although it was not yet seven she hugged herself and says, 'Let's go to bed.' You watched as she undressed and lay naked across the unmade sheets, her knees bent at the end of the bed and her feet inches from the floor. You knelt in front of her and kissed the inside of her thigh and found there was no warmth to her at all.

'I'm bleeding,' she says, and you could feel her hands gently steer your head. But you wouldn't let yourself be steered and your mouth filled with the taste of iron. After, she slept, her breathing shallow and dangerous. You blinked at the moonlight that came past the open curtain and fell across the cooling sheets.

34

In the morning, it had begun to rain outside; you could hear it on the glass. Vera was turned away from you in the bed, and her body occasionally jerked like it was being pulled across rough ground. She was crying and trying not to cry. You pressed your hand on her bare shoulder and closed your eyes to help you think.

'Have you ever been to one of those places where the sky is blue, not just sometimes, but all the time?'

'Yes,' she says, after a lull, and you felt her arm fall casually across your leg. Her washed-out voice.

'Where's the best?'

'There is no best.'

'But you've travelled, you've seen places?'

'Yes, I have.'

'No one I know has ever gone anywhere.'

'You know me.'

'Do I?'

'You know enough.' She turned and reached over for the packet of cigarettes on the bedside table. 'You'll see places, Sonny. I promise.' And just then, you believed her.

'There are little towns on the Spanish coast, Italy too.' She'd stopped crying. 'You wake up and go outside barefoot, and the ground warms your feet. In Morocco, there's this town.' She closed her eyes to remember. 'What's it called? Small fishing boats would come in with the catch, the whole town goes to meet them, and they light little fires on the beach, and for a few pennies they'll cook up the fish for you, you just point to the one you want. And you go, sit in the shade . . . You look out, and I swear, that sea, that great sea.'

As you stroked her face then you could feel the heat from her cheeks. Her wet eyelashes.

'I never wanted to live in Ireland.'

'I never wanted to live in Ireland either, but I'm not crying about it.'

'Thanks.' She leaned in towards you, to kiss you, you thought, but she didn't kiss you. She whispered instead, 'I need toast before I can screw again.' And taking hold of her robe, left you alone in the room.

Through your bones you could hear your own heart beat in your chest, steady. You wondered how long you could hold on to your breath. Less than a minute, and even if you wanted to hold it for longer, your body would just push your mind aside, and your lungs would fill up again with precious air. You knew; you'd tried it.

Downstairs she could just be heard and it comforted you, that sound of her. The house was otherwise so still, no post came, and the doorbell was never pressed. It was a long time before she came back to the bedroom. You were asleep and awake, and you knew she was there because you could feel the heat of her mouth cover you. Her feet were cold, as if she'd been walking barefoot in Belgrave Square, her white nightgown billowing.

★ ★ ★

In the afternoon, the phone rang. It made an awful urgent sound as it demanded Vera's attention. She raised herself up from the bed on her elbow, listening in disbelief. She might have let it ring off if you had not stupidly said, 'Don't answer it.' She looked at you first and then swung her legs over the side of the bed and disappeared quickly from the room.

'Hello,' you heard her say downstairs without a hint of surprise or apprehension. 'Oh, Brian, it's you . . . ' She stopped then. Dr Kelly had not called for a chat or to ask after her health. He had called to tell her things and to tell her off for palling around with youngsters who interfere. After a short time Vera was apologising, something about an imposition. He'd been very good and she was very sorry. 'Goodbye,' she says. 'I'm sorry, of course, and goodbye.' Then the clunky sound of the receiver being dropped back on its hook.

You waited to see if she was coming back, but there was only silence, endless amounts of it. You dressed quickly and from the balcony saw her sitting at the base of the stairs, her knees drawn in and her head resting forward. She must have felt each step as you came closer and crouched down beside her.

'I'm sorry,' you say and pressed your hand on the small of her back.

'Don't,' she says. 'What did I ask you, what was the one thing?' She rubbed her forehead. 'He was my last ally in Dublin. The last one.'

'You have me,' you say and in the second it took for her to look at you, you wished you had not.

'You need to leave now, darling,' she says.

'I don't want to.'

'I need some time to think.'

'OK,' you say, about to stand, but stopped with your face close to hers. 'I'll come back later.'

'Don't.'

'Please.'

'I'll . . . telephone you.'

'We don't have the phone in.'

'You need to leave, now.'

35

At home everything had got smaller again. From the moment you passed through the door into the cramped hallway and further, into the living room and kitchen, it had become an overstuffed doll's house. You had mostly forgotten about school, but being in the house reminded you. They would be in touch soon; you didn't know how or when, but some official record would be needed. You imagined the principal pulling up outside, checking the address on the piece of paper in his hand, before stepping from the car in the hope that there would be no shouting or threats after he'd delivered the news. But your family wasn't like that, they would never shout at him. They were decent, your family. They would apologise and feel ashamed of the worn patch of carpet at the front door near the principal's feet, because when asked in he would have refused and stood somewhere between coming inside and standing out on the step.

The principal didn't arrive. He sent a typed note with the school's bold emblem on the top. It said Graeme had been savagely beaten.

It said Graeme was a good boy. It said his only regret was that Graeme's family could not be encouraged to press charges. It said that you were not welcome back nor were you ever welcome on the school grounds at any time.

After the letter had passed around the hands of the family it was your father's turn. A space was cleared for him at the kitchen table but he could not find his glasses, pink glasses that had a single arm and used to belong to your mother. He set about checking under pillows and on the mantel behind the clock. Finally a brother saw them on a shelf on the kitchen dresser, but because he hadn't talked to your father in years, he could only say, 'Mam,' and point. Your mother picked them off the shelf and put them down on the table beside the letter.

'Tell your father his glasses are here,' she says to you. He came up off his knees where he had been searching under the couch and put them on.

There was a smirk behind his back that encouraged another smirk. He was a lumbering giant, thwarted by the clean lines of writing, and his lips tried to fold around the words, stumbling and starting again. You listened cautiously to the conversation as it fell around you. Then somehow Vera's name was mentioned and mentioned again; by the time your father put the letter back on the table, it was her fault. You'd been fine until you'd met her. You'd been a nice boy, quiet. Now you were ruined and she'd been your ruination. You saw that they were helping your father, so he'd know how to react to the letter, so he wouldn't get it wrong and get angry about how you'd beaten that boy, or that you'd never be schooled again.

Your mother says, 'That's that. He'll just have to stop seeing her, she'll have to be told to leave him alone,' then your father rose from the table, pulling the glasses from his face. He understood. You felt his hand on your back, pushing you towards the door, into the night air.

In the van he was silent. He revved the engine and tore away from the path. After he'd turned the corner the van slowed and he seemed worried.

'What are you going to do?' you say. The dashboard lit some of his face, showed his age and added more. Some years later, when he died, he would be buried without you ever touching that face.

'I'm going to tell her to leave well alone.' He was growling, but there was nothing in it.

'It's not her fault,' you say. 'You know that.' He was silent. The car turned the corner towards Dun Laoghaire.

'You don't have to, just because she tells you.' Your voice was small against the sound of the engine, but not so small that he didn't hear you.

'That's enough outta you,' he says. When he exhaled his air was jagged and his hand brushed past your knee, searching in the glove compartment for smokes.

'I'll get them,' you say after he veered for a moment towards oncoming cars. You reached in and found a packet of Gold Bond and saw that there were three full cigarettes and one half smoked. You took a full one and lit it, inhaled deeply, and when you passed it to him, he clenched it between his fingers.

Outside Vera's house he turned to you. 'Do you want to stay there or come in or what?' You slowly opened your door and stepped out of the van. He was already up the steps. You looked over the house and found comfort in knowing she was somewhere inside.

He didn't ring the bell, but smashed his huge fist three times on the door. Vera appeared at the top-floor window seen only by you. An outline of her behind the glass. When your father thumped on the door again, her shoulders flinched.

'She's not home. Leave it. Just leave it,' you shout. Then, softer: 'Go home and leave the woman in peace, for God's sake.' Vera had moved away from the window, and though your father's hand rose to the door again, you knew it would fall back. He glanced at the empty windows before turning to you.

'Get in the van,' he says and walked towards it.

'I'm staying,' you say. 'Tell Ma you talked to her, you fixed it, and that I ran off or something.' He considered the struggle to get you in the van. Even for her, he was not willing. He put his hand on the bonnet and looked away down the empty street. Once inside, his face disappeared into the blackness; he revved once, and you shut your eyes.

The quiet night overwhelmed you. You rang the bell and called her name through the letterbox. It took a long time before the door opened.

'I'm speechless,' she says. 'I can't imagine who will show up at my door next. Why was your father here?'

'He wanted to let you know me ma is coming later.' But she didn't laugh; she put her forehead against the door.

'Sonny, why was your father here?'

'I was expelled last week.'

'You never said.'

'No.'

'Come in, come in,' she says, and you followed her upstairs.

It was over; even you knew it was over, but like one of those big trawlers it took miles of ocean to stop. You were losing her, as she lay for hours, asleep, awake.

'I'm sorry,' she says. 'It's not fair, what I'm doing to you.' You ran your cold fingers through her hair and round to stroke the skin at the back of her neck. She let out the gentlest moan.

'I love you, Vera, I really do.'

'Oh, darling,' she says then. 'This isn't love. You need to know that.' But you knew what you felt.

'You've been so good to me, Sonny. I hadn't expected it, these feelings for you.'

'I'm glad,' you say, but you were disappointed even at that. Her affections for you were a tepid thing and though that should have made it easier for you to let go of her, it didn't.

'I'm freezing,' she says.

'Do you want me to light a fire?'

'There's no coal — I refused delivery.'

So you plugged in the electric heater and its glow illuminated the floor around it.

Later, when your bodies had warmed and you were a little drunk, you lay naked across her and asked her to say I love you, so you could hear it once, but she pushed you aside, rose up on her hands and knees and told you to fuck her that way, hard. So you did, and before you finished, you pulled her hair into your fist and whispered, 'I fucking hate you.'

36

The electric heater fought hard, but still pockets of cold air collected just a few feet from its light. You must have slept and woken and slept until morning. You remembered Vera's eyes open in the night, flickering, restless. Her mouth dry, opening and closing.

She reached over and rubbed her hand on your cheek and says, 'Let's have a nice day, let's go for a drive.'

She wore soft wool and some silk. You loved to watch her dress, all that desire in reverse, each bit of clothing slowly covering her skin. Then she walked to her bedside table and lifted a cut-glass bottle with a gold top, and she dabbed her neck once and both wrists. The room lifted with the smell of her.

She was passing through and what you had already seen would have to sustain you. You knew that even if she pressed against you, right then, that scent she left on your skin would fade.

You drove to Wicklow, had tea and sandwiches in a small pub in Delgany, where a coal fire smouldered at your side and Vera pretended to eat by breaking her sandwich into pieces and scattering them across her plate. She turned to you and over the barman's radio says, 'Well, almost made it through spring.' She put her hand on top of yours, and then quickly removed it.

'I saw the daffodils and tulips and even the carnations.' She smiled then. 'Though carnations are an atrocity. Sonny, one must make an effort for the fucking carnations.'

She rubbed her hands together and looked down at her white fingers.

'Let's stop by Greystones on the way back and walk the Strand,' she says. You stood and insisted on paying for the sandwich and tea against her protests, and to the barman's clear surprise she wrapped herself around you, and you felt the warm imprint of her lips on your cheek. It was the perfect end to your savings. You had nothing and felt free from it.

Outside, Vera lit a cigarette and tossed you the packet before stooping down into the little car. She smoked and changed gears like a truck driver. A pop song played on the radio, and it started to rain a little. The ineffectual wipers pushed the water from one side of the windscreen to the other and back again. You sat with your back pressed to your door and your body turned towards her as best the little seats would let you.

The car park at Greystones beach was

deserted, no one else to witness the heavy grey clouds pitched along the horizon. Later you would remember the sensation of the stones under your feet and somewhere a barking dog and the screaming of hungry gulls. The closed amusements and rusting shutters and you telling Vera, 'You're lovely, you are, just lovely.'

You hadn't walked for long before the cold shook you both, and you could see more rain being carried in across the Irish Sea. You made a dash for the car with her hand in yours; the stones skittered and Vera laughed as the first huge drops made ground around you. In the car the old leather seats creaked as Vera stretched towards you. Her hair and face were wet, and as she kissed you, you could feel her tongue deep in your mouth. She removed her tights and rolled up her skirt. You felt her exposed thighs when she sat across you. Ever so quietly you heard the words, 'I love you.' Mixed with the heat of her breath and so lightly that years later you would have to wonder if you'd made it up, and anyway, it didn't work; the seats were too close, and the car was too small, and after a few attempts with Vera's legs twisting towards the ridiculous, laughter took you both and you gave up.

★   ★   ★

You were caught in rush-hour traffic on the way back from Greystones. At a bottleneck junction in Dun Laoghaire, the car sat idle for nearly a half-hour, the lights from the shopping centre cutting across Vera's face. At Eason's bus stop a large crowd gathered, and you sat watching them as more and more late-night shoppers joined the ranks. You began to fret for the ones at the end who would never make it onto the bus. Vera had not said a word since Bray. She had slid back into that secret place where she went and would or could not share with you.

Once home she'd gone directly to the kitchen and from the front door you heard the sound of her keys dropping onto the table. You found her seated, head down, her fingers slowly combing through her hair. You hovered close until she looked up, and though you were right there, it took some time for her eyes to locate you, and even then they lay across you so lightly.

'Let's get drunk,' she says. She smiled a bit.

'Are you sure you want to?'

'I am sure.' And she sat up and banged her hands on the table. 'Let's get fucking locked . . . What's left?'

You checked the presses where she kept the wine.

'One bottle of red wine, two onions and a carrot.'

'Well, that's hardly enough for a stew.'

You opened the wine bottle and she stood and searched the kitchen and you saw how she stayed away from the drawer that housed her tablets. An almost-full bottle of whiskey was located and poured neat into two tumblers. It was harsh at first and you could feel your body reject it until subdued by the alcohol and you were drunk. You sat at the table and clinked glasses and smoked. When you said the mix of wine and whiskey would give an awful hangover in the morning, she says, 'Fuck the morning.'

She paced herself and filled your glass and you knew and you let her. You reached over and took her hand and watched as your thumb moved over her fingers. And you drank and drank until tears filled your eyes and she helped you to bed.

You remembered that during the night she pushed back into you, in the sleepy way she had before, and you wrapped your arms about her and held her tight in a way that made you almost believe you had succeeded for her.

★ ★ ★

In the morning she lay still under the blankets, the little bedside lamp burning against the natural light. She had undressed, and her clothes lay neatly draped over the wooden chair. Underneath her dressing gown she had on an old pair of pyjamas you had never seen. She'd thought it through, considered what clothes she was comfortable having on when her body was discovered by men in heavy boots who would bang up and down the stairs, calling loudly to each other.

The ambulance men did come for her. You stood over them, watching as they removed her body carefully from the bed and onto the stretcher. She was not dead, but almost. They hadn't believed your story, that you'd come to work that morning and found her that way. The guards would probably be in touch, they said, but they were clear it was not their business what had gone on the night before.

'Jaysus, first time's unlucky, second is just careless, wha'?' you heard one say to the other going down the stairs. They had remembered you from before.

You tried to piece it together yourself, after you'd woken up, and it was light, and your head thumped. It was then you noticed how still she was, how her breaths were shallow and vague, and her skin was pale. You called her name, gently at first, then louder and shaking her whole body. She was there and gone all at once. You had been the one to call the ambulance, and she would never have forgiven you for that.

262

37

After the ambulance left, taking Vera with it, only that awful silence remained in the big empty house. You only held on a while, thinking to smooth the gathered sheets, to remove the shape your bodies had made together. But you stood at the end of the bed and could not and so pulled the front door shut, locked it, posted the keys into the letterbox and walked to St Michael's.

The hospital stood back from the main Dun Laoghaire road but not so much that patients near the window wouldn't hear the constant sound of traffic rising up.

You couldn't go inside at all, you couldn't face it. There was a little brick wall at the front, and you sat on that wall, watching the windows and the ambulances coming and going and the doctors and the nurses and all the caring relatives carrying flowers and spare pyjamas and boxes of chocolates and you didn't know if Vera was dead or if machines had been brought to her side, and they were pumping and bleeping and doing that cold job of saving her life so she could come through to die all over again.

It would have happened at the same quick pace, opening the tablets, pouring them out, putting them into her mouth. And then filling her mouth with water so cold it would have hurt her teeth. She must have walked up the stairs after she was done, so frightened as she lay in the bed next to you and covered herself with the blanket and waited. The terrible loneliness of that waiting.

You didn't notice it getting dark. You stood and walked towards the main door, where there was a dim light at the entrance, but again you were unable to go inside. You'd failed her.

'Have you a light, young fella?' came a voice to your left; you turned and saw an old woman holding a plastic shopping bag in one hand. In the other, a cigarette, pointed at your nose.

'Yes, I do,' you say, and found your voice was normal.

'Sure you're all right, I have one myself, I was only making chat. Do you know? Have you got one in there?'

'What?'

'Inside, one of yours in there?' Her face was half covered in the kind of headscarf that old women wore when they'd had their hair set. Your ma had one, but it was plain beside this woman's.

'Yes,' you say.

'Poor thing, your da, is it?'

'No.'

'Surprised, it's usually the das go first. Your mam?'

'No.'

'Well, that's good news, anyway.'

She lit her cigarette. The smoke disappeared inside her and never returned.

'Sorry, do you want one?'

'Thanks, I'm all right. I just had one.'

'Mine's in there, husband, angina, a triple bypass. I mean, what's the point? I mean, if he'd just pass I could go home. Living here now, over the years, I couldn't tell you what he's waiting for anyway, he does nothing. All the nurses know me. I bring them things, home-made jam and that, even that Paki doctor says hello to me now, and he talks to no one. You're quiet — are you sure you won't have a smoke? Go on, it'll do you good.'

You took a cigarette, and when you drew on it, it made you feel sick, and you were exhausted. You saw you could do ordinary things, that that was the way it was with you. You could smoke a smoke with a stranger and chat too. You'd sleep and eat and shit and fuck. And just then your whole body folded in two, and your eyes were saturated, and the old woman was saying, 'Christ, young fella, are you all right? Will I call someone for you?'

You could hear her shouting for somebody to help you. Her voice had become muffled, a faraway sound. You pulled back from the hospital entrance, and your walk became a run, and shop lights and car lights and street lights all blurred.

38

Your ma seemed content to have you back. 'I don't want to know,' she says. 'I just don't want to know.' But you had offered nothing.

She had taken it on herself to go and see Joe. She made promises on your behalf, and Joe had agreed to give you a start. You'd have to go up to the tech two mornings a week and do extra hours up with Joe and Mick right away. There was a lot of talk about 'Not wrecking your chances,' and 'It's a good opportunity you were given,' and 'There's a lot of young lads out there would be only too happy to take your place.'

Minutes passed in blocks, like concrete, like grey chunks of time. You stayed up late with your father, watching an old picture, the room in a fog of cigarette smoke. When it was over, he stood and walked in his heavy way to turn on the light and unplug the telly. Then bent to pick up his tea-stained cup and leave it in the sink for your ma in the morning. There was a word like 'goodnight'. You sat then, in the silent house with the white ash that covered the cooling fire, rubbing your face and finding a way to bed.

The next morning you took the bus to the tech, its heavy diesel engine billowing black smoke, and it came to a standing stop outside St Michael's hospital. You sat behind its vibrating glass feeling the weight of every brick and broken body. Not daring to look left or right and knowing that if you did, the pull of her gravity would knock you off course.

At the tech, you sat beside Bricks O'Toole, who smelt of cheese-and-onion crisps and had hands filled with scars. You were given textbooks that neither of you read. Pages were dog-eared and missing, filled with boys' drawings of spurting pricks and football teams. Bricks told you that as long as you showed up most of the time you'd pass, that they didn't give a shit if you could cut up a bleeden' cow. Besides, he said, he didn't give a bollox anyway; he was going out on the container ships as soon as his court case was heard. 'They'd take fucking anyone on the ships,' he says. He'd bitten a fella's ear off in a fight, and he was told if he enrolled in a course, the judge would go easy. You heard later that he'd been given eight months in Mountjoy. Grievous bodily harm.

You couldn't take the bus back to the butcher shop, past the hospital a second time in a single day, so you walked the long way round.

'Are you late, are you bleeden' late back on your first day?' says Mick, holding his wristwatch in the air. 'The class only takes two hours, and look it, the time.' You said you were sorry, that the bus had broken down. He didn't believe you.

There wasn't much for you to do, you weren't to be trusted with the cuts, and Joe and Mick were already falling over each other to serve the few customers that did come in. So you cleaned the mincer and boiled the kettle and made mugs of tea that went cold.

'You wanna go for a pint?' says Mick, at the end of the day, the shutter already closed. You were confused at first; he'd asked you in the same voice he used to give you a telling-off.

'A wha'?'

'A pint. I bring the apprentice for a pint the first day, so I do — you want a fucking pint or not?'

'Yeah . . . thanks.'

You waited for him to put the locks on the gates and walked in silence to the pub. Inside, it was warm; there was a loud song playing and you knew some faces from around, but not well enough to say hello. At the bar, Mick ordered two pints and made a gesture about them being on him. He took a gulp from his beer and wiped his face with the back of his hand and his eyes darted quickly around the room. He looked on the verge of being excited and you felt somehow that when he looked at you, you were draining that excitement. When his face turned away you imagined him rolling his eyes and thinking it would be a long pint.

'I'm going for a slash,' he says. 'And for fuck's sake, Sonny, cheer up the fuck, would you?'

You had never stood at a bar on your own, and taking a sip of your drink you felt very unsure. You watched the barman work and then saw yourself in the mirror behind him. The faces, the soft light and the cracks of laughter as people held on to each other with affection, and for years this would stay with you and you wished you could be another you and stay and know belonging.

Over your shoulder then, past the drift of smoke, was Sharon. She never drank, yet there she was sitting with a pint of cider and some older fella beside her talking to her da. In the mirror she caught your eye, scowled a bit and gave you the finger. She grinned when you walked over and she held her lit smoke unnaturally high as if showing it off.

'Sonny,' she says, loud. 'Jaysus, what happened to you, did the sun stop shining on the Monkstown Road?'

'Mick asked me to come for a drink.'

'Oh, so you're going to be a butcher after all?' She was like a stranger to you then; you searched beyond her drunkenness, beyond the heavy cover of her make-up and the thick mascara around her eyes that looked like it had bled once and dried.

As if she was playing hide-and-seek with you, not here, not here. 'You must be chuffed,' she says and laughed. She lifted her drink from the table and took it down in big mouthfuls.

'We're celebrating ourselves,' she says and then you saw what she had been trying to show you all along. A large diamond ring on her wedding finger. 'Aren't we, Jim, aren't we?' But Jim was turned to her da just then, not wanting to be bothered. 'Jim?' she says. 'We're celebrating, aren't we?'

'Yeah,' Jim says over his shoulder. 'Celebrating.'

'We're getting married,' says Sharon, again holding up her hand. 'It's not real or nothing, it's a temporary one till we get a real one, that's what people do. Isn't it, Jim, Jim? And we're on the list for a house up in Ballyboden, you know there?'

'No.'

'It's great, isn't it, Jim? Jaysus, Jim?'

'Great,' says Jim, turning then, putting his arm around Sharon's neck and pulling her close, kissing her cheek while looking at you. He had a moustache and rolled-up sleeves; the underarms of his purple silk shirt were stained.

'And who are you?' he says.

'Sonny.'

'Sonny,' he says, and turned to Sharon. 'Friend of yours?'

Sharon looked at you. 'Well, Sonny? Are you a friend of mine?'

Mick had emerged from the toilet and was walking back across the pub. He saw the empty place at the bar where he'd left you, and sauntered forward unfazed.

'Yeah,' you say.

'Sonny's very highfalutin, aren't you? He goes to the National Gallery and all. He fancies a posh lady, don't you, an old one?' Jim had put his hand across Sharon's belly then and was rubbing at it, back and forth; there was something you found grotesque about his hands and their movement. Back and forth, back and forth; you felt further drained by each stroke.

'Well, congratulations,' you say, taking a first step back towards where Mick stood at the bar.

'Did it not work out with your one, then?' she says.

'What? No, I mean, it — '

'Sure I could have told you that.'

'He going to keep rubbing your belly like that? Thinks it's Aladdin's fucking lamp he has there.'

'Wha'?' says Jim. 'Do you know who you're talking to?'

'It's all right, Jim,' says Sharon. 'Sure he's fucking nothing, aren't you? You'll never be anything, Sonny, you'll never be a man, not one that's any use anyway.' And Sharon put her hand on top of Jim's.

'You'd wanna leave now,' says Jim to his side, his eyes flicking up towards you. You looked away, back through the smoke to where Mick was sitting. He was watching you then, he tapped his finger on his wrist where a watch might be, drained his pint and turned back towards the barman. Sharon put her thumb to her mouth, and started to bite it absent-mindedly, then remembered and put it down by her side, and as you made your way out of the pub that filled you with affection.

39

You walked directly from the pub to the hospital. The walk seemed to do your body good and even the invisible rain that soaked you through couldn't take away what had opened inside of you, quite suddenly.

You went to the reception area and to the front desk, past the shapes of strangers who were moving with great purpose and bowed serious heads. There was a stout matron behind the counter, with a little watch clipped above the breast of her uniform. She held several large folders balanced up the length of her forearms; they looked heavy, but she showed no sign of it.

She had caught your eye when you first walked in, but just then it didn't suit her. So you waited, and your confidence waned only a little.

'I'm here to see Vera Hatton, please,' you say, and at that name, the matron blinked and took an interest in you.

'Just a moment.' She went to her colleague. 'He's here to see Vera Hatton.' You could plainly hear her say it. The second matron stopped what she was doing and turned, and they both stared at you.

'If you can come this way,' the first matron says, moving around the counter and leading you down the corridor, her hands pressed tightly together.

'You are related to the patient?' You could hear her country accent then. She was being delicate.

'I'm her nephew,' you say.

'Oh, I see,' she says. 'Well, aren't you very good. You do know the conditions under which Mrs Hatton was brought to us?'

'I do,' you say. She looked away from you then, along the corridor as if something had caught her eye. She was embarrassed to tell you the awful thing of your aunt's condition.

'It's not the first time she's been here with us. We know her, we're all very fond of her, of course. She's in a coma. We don't know, well, we don't think . . . It's very serious, you should understand that?'

'I do.'

'Well, look, sure, it might be very good for you to see her, to talk to her and that, they say that helps. I'll call up and have them expect you — it's the third floor . . . ?

'Sonny.'

'Right, so, Sonny, go up, the doctor won't be back in until morning, but you can have a word if you like then. The lift is just there, you see it? Right, so. Good.'

You waited a long time for the door of the lift to open. You could hear the metal cage clunking slowly between floors, and stood next to a man holding a bouquet of flowers like they were a lump hammer. His lips were moving as if working over a row he'd lost. He got off on the second floor, and the doors closed, and you felt the atmosphere of the place press down.

When the lift opened again, a young nurse stood waiting.

'You're here for Vera?' she says. You nodded, yes. 'If you come this way,' she says. You followed, staying a few paces behind her, past the nurses' station, where one nurse sat, taking tea, and further down the corridor, past the dimly lit wards, with beds like ghost ships.

'Now, you might get a fright when you see her, with all the stuff, the tubes and that, but you don't need to worry, we've made her very comfortable. I like to warn people ahead of time, to prepare them. They often thank me after . . . just here now.' She stopped at a door.

'Would you like me to come in with you?'

'No. Thank you.'

Already through the glass square you could make out the shape of her body under the tightly pulled sheets. You had to push hard against the door to open it, and it closed quickly behind you. There was a machine beside Vera's bed, like the screen of a TV, with lines that swept across and jumped when Vera's heart beat.

Her face no longer matched your memory of it, something was absent. It was not like she was asleep; the wonder and curiosity had been suspended, and what remained frightened you. Her mouth had drooped to one side, and her chin was set across her chest and looked unnatural.

You didn't know what to do then. You thought to reach over and touch her. Her skin had a waxy whiteness. This was the difference, the few capsules you'd saved her from.

You sat and watched the rise and fall of her chest and even an occasional flicker under her eyes. You looked at the screen, bleeping and showing numbers that for a moment you thought you understood. Beep, beep, beep. There was hardly another sound in the world, save a nurse passing outside the door with gentle quick steps, the lift arriving and departing at the end of the corridor. At the nurses' station a phone would ring, but not often.

You reached over and took her hand. It wasn't cold to touch or anything, but there was no life to it. You thought you should cry, but there were no tears. You even kissed her hand and put your head against her lap and felt the crisp sheets beneath your ear, then sat back in the chair, watching, Vera and you, adrift, neither here nor there.

★   ★   ★

Later, there was a gentle tap-tapping at the door before it pushed open, and the nurse was there holding a tray. You stood up when she came in.

'I thought a little cuppa might be needed in here,' she says. You saw how she'd brought a pot of tea and some biscuits on a small plate.

'Thank you, thank you very much,' you say. She walked to Vera's bedside then. 'And how is our patient feeling?' She stroked Vera's face in an easy way. 'Look it, now, Vera, here's your nephew come all the way up from Wexford to see you. Isn't that great?' She spoke to her the way you'd talk to a child. 'I'll come back and get that tray from you a little later, and as a matter of fact there are some flowers down the way that are going to waste — I'll bring them back in when I'm coming, brighten the room a bit.' She looked at Vera again. 'Isn't she the most beautiful woman, I mean, you should have been in the films. Isn't that right now, Vera?' she says. And making her way to the door then: 'If there's anything you need, you let me know.'

'Thanks,' you say.

'That's all right, sure it's good to see her have a visitor. Bye for now, Vera.'

She had already turned and had a hand on the door when you asked, 'Does nobody come?'

She looked away from you when she spoke, as if embarrassed to say. 'No, not one, not as long as I've known her and I've known her a while now. We'd always offer to call someone for her, but no.'

'I didn't know she'd been sick that long.'

She stepped back inside the room, folded her arms and stood looking over the bed. You saw there was nowhere she was expected.

'I tell you something, I've a lot of patients that would come and go, but there was always something very special with Vera. I'm so fond of her — course I shouldn't play favourites. Do you know, every time we've discharged her, within a week flowers and chocolates would show and she knew every single person who worked on this floor by name. But I'll be honest with you, it's heartbreaking, every time she'd leave the hospital, you knew she'd be back. You just knew.'

'There's no cure, right?'

'Well, no, that's not true, there are very

successful treatments. I mean, this country is in the dark ages when it comes to depression, but even still. I often thought she'd do well to go back to England, seek help there, but I'd never say. She's a very private woman as I'm sure you know.'

'Yes, but for motor neurones, I was told there was no cure for motor neurones anywhere.' And you felt suddenly hopeful, that there was a chance, that if she recovered from this, there were treatments she might have overlooked or not asked about because she was so private and not wanting to impose.

It took you a moment to notice the nurse's face had changed and she was looking at you anew. 'It was her young lad had motor neurones, not Vera.'

'Her young lad?'

'Yes, her son, about your age. Sorry, was I right in thinking you're her nephew?'

'Yes,' you say, 'yes, of course.'

'Well, right. I don't want to be saying anything I shouldn't be saying, is all.'

'Of course.'

'I'll come back and get that tray after.' She left then, the door pulled closed, and from the base of her bed Vera's words gathered around you like fallen angels, naked for the first time. You draped your hand across her blanket, her body still warm beneath.

40

It was late, late enough to be called early. The nurse had come back since and collected the tray and as promised brought a small bunch of carnations. She said, 'Now,' and 'That's better and bye for now,' but wasn't inclined to chat in the same way. There wasn't a soul along the Dun Laoghaire main street when you looked out of Vera's window. And there was Vera and her sentinel's steady beep. You didn't know what to do. You climbed onto the hospital bed, putting your head close to hers. You thought how it would be to have her turn to you just then as you ran your fingers along her cheek and chin. She didn't smell like Vera any more; she'd been scrubbed and made sterile. You reached across and clamped your hand over her mouth and pressed her nostrils together. Her body began to shudder and then violently lurch forward. You could feel the heat of her mouth and even her wet spit under your hand. Her eyes never opened. It was a long time before her body was still. The screen's horizontal line flattened and sounded the alarm. You lay there, beside her, ready to be discovered. You moved your hand softly over her face and you didn't care when tears came. You kissed her a last time and her mouth wasn't cold the way they say; she wasn't peaceful either.

You were surrounded then. There were two, maybe three, nurses in the room and a doctor too. A nurse took you by the hand saying, 'It's OK,' and led you out to the hall. She stood with you by the door and pressed her hand on your arm and when she saw a nurse looking at her watch inside the room she says, 'Thank God she had someone with her, she didn't have to do it all alone.' But you didn't like her hand on you and moved away.

★　★　★

Outside, you walked without direction, watching for the dawn, to pull the night asunder.

When you reached Seapoint, the morning trains could be heard behind you and in front, granite steps ran into the sea. You held on to the thick rusted handrail and climbed down and put a first foot in the icy water. Then you waded out into the gentle lapping waves. You felt your legs scorching, then your balls and prick, your belly. You plunged headlong into the brown-grey sea. Holding your breath, the sudden silence. You could taste the salt at your lips and held your breath for as long as you could, and for a moment you were between worlds, before being thrown from the water, fighting for that precious air.

Acknowledgements

To my own brothers, who thankfully are not 'the brothers', my sisters too, for all your generosity and kindness, I am for ever grateful.

My friends from the best room in NYC, Dermot Burke, Tony Caffery Natilie Walsh, Brendan O'Shea, Francesca Fallaci. Brendan Byrne. And the mighty Asidro.

Evan Elizabeth Harder, David Winner, Micheal Almereyda, Geoffrey O'Sullivan, Bara Jichova Tyson, Deborah Clifford, Jenna Nicholls, Mark & Jess Connell, Davian Littlefield, Colin Brodrick, Jt Petty.

Joby Hickey, Grace Weir, Joe Walker, Nick Miller. Sinead Dolan, Paul Ferriter, Fionn Davenport, Emer Reynolds, Ness Evans, and the Fraser family.

Anna Stein, Sophie Lambert, Jonathan Lee. Kate Harvey and all at Harvill Secker.

To those waiting in the wings, Mum and Dad

and my great friends, Adam Roth and Frank Deasy.

And of course, my two angels, Billy and Lila.

We do hope that you have enjoyed reading this large print book.

Did you know that all of our titles are available for purchase?

We publish a wide range of high quality large print books including:
Romances, Mysteries, Classics
General Fiction
Non Fiction and Westerns

Special interest titles available in large print are:
The Little Oxford Dictionary
Music Book
Song Book
Hymn Book
Service Book

Also available from us courtesy of Oxford University Press:
Young Readers' Dictionary
(large print edition)
Young Readers' Thesaurus
(large print edition)

For further information or a free brochure, please contact us at:
Ulverscroft Large Print Books Ltd.,
The Green, Bradgate Road, Anstey,
Leicester, LE7 7FU, England.
Tel: (00 44) 0116 236 4325
Fax: (00 44) 0116 234 0205